hellscapes
volume 1

hellscapes
volume 1

stephen zimmer

SEVENTH STAR PRESS

Cover art: Matthew Perry
Cover art in this book copyright © 2013 Matthew Perry & Seventh Star
Press, LLC.

Editor: Rodney Carlstrom

Published by Seventh Star Press, LLC.

ISBN Number: 978-1-937929-36-7

Seventh Star Press
www.seventhstarpress.com
info@seventhstarpress.com

Publisher's Note:
Hellscapes, Volume 1 is a work of fiction. All names, characters, and
places are the product of the author's imagination, used in fictitious
manner. Any resemblances to actual persons, places, locales, events,
etc. are purely coincidental.

Printed in the United States of America

First Edition

ACKNOWLEDGEMENTS

I would like to thank my mother and father, though both have left this world behind I never would have been able to pursue the path I have were it not for their encouragement, support, and love. The deeper the love, the deeper the pain, and I endure my own kind of Hellscape in the time left to me in a world where the shadows thrive far too often. But my eyes look farther ahead.

Rodney Carlstrom, my steadfast editor on this project, who did not shy away from the darker explorations in this journey. Insights and suggestions delivered in Rodney's trademark style led to a stronger finished work. A good editor watches out for an author, and Rodney certainly did.

Matthew Perry, another who has endured the long-suffering road of pursuing dreams. I am always honored to have Matt's artwork gracing the covers and interiors of my books. I'm just glad I could finally get something out in the pure horror genre, which I know Matt is happy about!

I would like to thank the readers near, far, and wide, who give me that second wind whenever I'm tiring, and who prop me up if I begin to stumble. I never for a second forget that authors are nothing without readers, and I want all my readers to know that I give them my very best with every work I put forth.

I deeply appreciate my Seventh Star Press family, a refuge in a difficult world. It is wonderful to have companions to share the journey with.

DEDICATION

To the One Who shows a Way by which all can escape the grasp of dark realms

To my mother and father, two celestial lights that no darkness could ever dim.

THE TALES

WELCOME TO THE HELLSCAPES

Many readers of my epic fantasy series, Fires in Eden, and urban fantasy series, The Rising Dawn Saga, might be a little surprised at this first installment of the Hellscapes. To me, this is something that's been a long time in coming.

I've always loved the horror genre, a wonderful member of the speculative fiction family. In fact, one of my biggest author inspirations is the amazing, multi-talented Clive Barker (whose artwork and movies I've also drawn a great deal of inspiration from). Authors such as Clive Barker show the range and possibilities in horror, which can explore some areas that other genres can't reach as effectively.

I've had many hints of the horror part of my background throughout my other work. The Rising Dawn Saga, with its depictions of the Ten-Fold Kingdom of Diabolos, most certainly has many scenes and moments with horror elements. In my Fires in Eden series, beings such as the Arcamons and the fiery realms of Jebaalos contain a host of horror aspects.

I do have one published short story, "The Excavation", in the Vampires Don't Sparkle anthology put together and edited by a truly top-flight horror author himself, Michael West. That was a bit of a kickoff for me, but the Hellscapes represents my first dedicated book release in the genre.

The name for the collection, Hellscapes, says it all as far as the theme of these stories. The setting and environments for all of the stories to be found this this volume and subsequent ones is the Infernal. The stories, for the most part, involve various souls who are arriving in this horrific part of the afterlife, though in most instances they have no initial awareness of where they are or how they got there.

Depending on what kind of individual they were in their mortal life, they find themselves in situations and places well-suited to their particular past. The stories can get very visceral, and shocking to a degree, but there is always a method to the madness. Many evils of our world can be explored in a vivid manner within this kind of story writing, with no holds barred.

Looking back at the first group of stories, I see my love of Dante's *Inferno*, Milton's *Paradise Lost*, and Clive Barker reflected in the kinds of tones to be found within. Some stories are more fantastical than others, and some are more gruesome, but all of them show the things of

WELCOME TO THE HELLSCAPES

the darkness for what they are.

Welcome to the Hellscapes! Buckle up and enjoy the ride into places fascinating to visit, but defnitely not pleasant to live in!

-Stephen Zimmer
September 2, 2013

BLOOD DREAMS

BLOOD DREAMS

"There is no dignity in wickedness, whether in purple or rags; and hell is a democracy of devils, where all are equals."
-Herman Melville

Blood dreams, rising from the depths of a crimson sea. Macabre symphonies beckoning without cessation, calling with timeless grandeur to a shadow-dance unending. Yearning lusts intertwining with raging vengeance, a burning seduction into a fathomless darkness.

Awakening from infernal slumber, the Entity gloried in the embrace of hungers sated. Furies relished with promises of realization; limitless possibilities swirled within nightmare dominions.

Thoughts lingered upon another world, a place of time and space grasping towards a long-sought harmony with the infernal realms. Filling with cold winds and cries of the lost, a globe being draped with the shroud of hell's victory awaited its approaching doom.

Boasting godhead and surrendering to oblivion, flesh and blood images shunned the Source with defiant pride. Reflections of an ageless rebellion, the condemned brimmed with the rapturous ecstasy of final damnation. No longer with eyes to see, they were also bereft of ears to hear.

Currents of sorrow buoyed the Entity taking flight, soaring across horizons of abandoned hope. Like a shining light consumed within the maw of impenetrable night, a long-anticipated soul had finally arrived; and the Entity savored every thought of the imminent welcoming.

***

Looking onward in stunned silence, Helen Carville beheld the grotesque parade with a consuming, rising dread. Stretching to the far horizon, naked forms of flesh were being dragged mercilessly across harsh ground riddled with shards of jagged, obsidian rock; the latter raking deep into their bloodied, shredded skin.

Black chains were fixed tight about their necks, and Helen could see the skin sizzling about the edges of the ebon links. The acrid stench of burning flesh carried to her on the hot currents of air, filling her with nausea and revulsion.

The hapless beings' tormentors were hulking brutes of great height, monstrous creatures with bestial countenances and lumbering strides. Their bodies were covered in scars, patches of fur, and oozing sores, as if they themselves had recently emerged from similarly terrible ordeals.

Eyes blazing with hate, they snarled and roared at the ill-fated captives. One of the gigantic beasts, gnashing its jagged teeth, abruptly swayed its gaze upon Helen, spiking the woman's heartbeat. Jaws widening, it loosed a bellowing roar, drawing the attention of several others of its brawny ilk towards her.

Looking to her left and right, Helen saw only an empty, barren plain. She did not know how she had arrived there, part of the dismaying predicament that she could remember nothing.

Her mind was steeped in a disorienting fog. Panic swelled as one of the monsters let go of the chains it held and took a purposeful step in her direction.

Behind the beast, at the other end of the dark chain, the barely recognizable form of a woman lay quivering. Her body was already ripped to tatters on the sharp, protruding edges of rock littering the pathway. There was no mistaking what the massive brute would do to Helen if it managed to get hold of her.

Unable to think of any alternative, and all of her instincts screaming danger, Helen fled into the wasteland spreading outward from the gore-streaked roadway. After a hundred yards, she chanced a quick look back, and saw no signs of pursuit. The monsters had all turned back to their grisly labors, dragging the hapless victims across the flesh-tearing surface.

Nevertheless, Helen pressed forward with haste, wishing she could recall at least something that would help her understand the dire circumstances she faced. Shreds and pieces of memory flitted through her mind; images of gala affairs, filled with smiling faces and the trappings of power. Visions of flashing lights and eager faces pranced before her inner sight; echoes of a time and place she knew was as good as illusion in the face of her arid, oppressive surroundings.

She kept pressing forward, though for how long she could not say. There were no changes in the ambiance to indicate the passing of time.

Roiling, reddish cloud layers flowed angrily in an unceasing procession across the upper skies. There was no sun in view, but there was more than enough luminance to see for a far distance.

Helen knew deep inside that an unnatural state surrounded her, though what it was she had no inkling. The feeling of dread continued to pervade her, harrying her every thought as she struggled to comprehend what was happening to her.

Farther and farther she walked across the featureless landscape. The scratches of her shoes upon the parched ground were the only sounds breaking the weighty, dead silence encompassing her. Not even a fragment of a breeze disturbed the still air.

Her every breath felt labored, each inhalation proving inadequate to assuage the demands of her lungs. Yet breathing faster did nothing to mitigate the discomfort she felt inside.

Helen's eyes lowered to the reddish, rocky soil underfoot. She fell into a kind of trance, watching her steps as she continued onward. Her mind slowly emptied of all thoughts, save for what was necessary to take one stride after another.

With no conception of how long she had been walking, Helen finally raised her eyes up from the ground. She blinked in surprise and flinched, taking in the sight of a host of new, prominent features.

Soaring up from the desolate plain were a teeming mass of great hills or mountains, looming dark sentinels warding the edge of the desert. Seeing something other than flat, rocky ground ahead, Helen started for the rises.

It never occurred to her that her muscles were not showing any trace of fatigue, despite the exertion and distance she had covered. With no impetus to slow down or take a respite, she pressed onward, willing herself to reach the dusky heights.

***

Helen gasped in shock a moment later, abruptly finding herself on the slopes of a mountain. Blinking rapidly, and breathing fast, she tried to make sense of what had just happened.

More pieces of memory came to her, enough to bring recognition of the place she now found herself in. Looking around, Helen found that she stood within a cemetery of the sort she had seen often in images beamed back by satellites and surveillance drones. The burial site could have been found within any number of countries ranging from the Middle East to Central Asia.

The air was no longer stagnant. Searing winds lashed the mountainside, whipping against her body with great force. She kept her legs planted firmly, bracing herself against the push of the invisible currents.

As she looked on, a strange sequence of events began to transpire. Like ascending columns of smoke, the ground in front of each grave marker began to swirl, and then climb skyward.

In moments, the outlines of grave pits were revealed, as the earth shook itself loose and coiled upwards. As the cavities steadily grew deeper, a spectral light began emitting from deeper within them.

Helen could not keep her eyes from the surreal spectacle, even if every part of her being cried out with warning, to get away from the area as fast as possible. She stood transfixed, compelled to witness whatever was about to manifest.

Dirt and debris flowed upward with increasing speed, and the light within each opening intensified. As the air above the cemetery filled with swirling dust, the area became filled with a dynamic cascade as the light rays filtered through the particles. The mesmerizing sight was as beautiful as it was haunting.

A deep chill seeped into Helen's body, as she saw pale, ghostly forms begin ascending from the grave pits. The partially translucent figures of men, women, and children of all ages floated out of the eerie luminance, and began drifting about the cemetery.

From their distinctive garb, and the long beards on many of the men, Helen suspected they were from one of the lands that had experienced the military might of the United States. Men in chapan coats, wearing lengthy garments called kameez, or shalwar, a type of baggy trouser, drifted alongside women dressed in either a distinctive style of ankle-length, colorful dresses, or another body-length dress called abaya.

The heads of every adult were covered, the men featuring an assortment of caps, such as the karakul and pakol, and the lungee, a type of turban. The women exhibited an array of head scarves and veils, including several with hijabs.

At first, none of the pallid specters took any notice of Helen. She continued watching them glide smoothly through the air, unaffected by the physical turbulence generated by the winds. Many more were emerging from the open graves, joining their number with the others already in the air above the cemetery.

Helen then took notice of several apparitions keeping

to the ground level, walking along the surface as if they had physical weight to their forms. A good number of those flying about began settling down upon the ground, after several more moments had passed.

Though every instinctive part of her screamed desperately to flee the place, Helen could not find the will to move. The unearthly scene captivated her attention, sapping her of initiative and resolve.

Helen looked to the right, and saw a child of about six or seven years of age only a few paces away. The child turned slowly towards Helen.

She recoiled as she set her eyes upon the little girl's rheumy eyes. The child's lips spread in a mockery of a smile, carrying the cold sneer of the pitiless. It was a look entirely devoid of humor, or any remote trace of good will.

Shards of terror lanced through Helen, seeing that all of the spirits were now gazing at her with similar, icy expressions. They began drawing closer to her, including a young woman in bridal attire who broke into a mirthless, sustained laughter that cut through the winds.

The sound took on a rough, grating edge as the woman neared Helen among the converging, ghostly throng. None of the figures she looked upon had pupils. All of them were like the child, having gazes in which the spark of life was conspicuously absent.

One by one, the figures began reaching out towards her. Their fingers were like shards of ice, frozen to the touch wherever they made contact with Helen's skin. Shrill laughter, like salutations of madness, filled her ears and shook her spirit.

Something told her that she was connected in some way to each and every one of the apparitions, from the most frail-looking elder to the youngest child. Out of the mists of memory, bits and pieces from the past started to come forward.

Her eyes drifted back towards the woman in traditional bridal garments. Their greenish hue indicated the religious ceremony involved in the marriages of their culture had not been completed when she had died.

The segments of memory then connected within Helen's mind, bringing clarity to an exercise of her authority that ended in blood and fire. A firestorm loosed from above had destroyed the impending union of a husband and wife, along with the lives of many others. Gathered on a day promising joy and celebration, they had all been taken up within a vicious eruption of flame and thunder.

Dismissed as a deeply regrettable mistake in the vacuous parlance of diplomats, the horror visited upon those assembled for the wedding became just another incident to be forgotten; in a world where the cries of the innocent rarely found an ear who would listen. Now, Helen found herself within a realm where nothing had been forgotten, and accountability was demanded.

Finding a sliver of her own willpower, she began

backing away from the groping shades, wondering how she had ever come to such an awful fate. The specters moved forward in the wake of her retreating steps, showing no sign at all of letting up in their pursuit.

Glancing over her shoulder, she froze in terror as she realized the heels of her shoes were at the cusp of a towering precipice. A dizzying drop over a thousand feet gaped mere inches behind her.

The ghostly hands clutched and pawed at her again, until finally she felt herself being shoved over the rocky lip. Helen could do nothing to resist the pressing throng, and tilting backwards she felt the weightlessness behind.

Her raw screams trailed her plummeting body. Helpless, she watched as the edge of the cliff grew smaller. Rushing down the jagged rock face, she knew that a bone-shattering collision between her body and the ground was imminent.

***

Shaking and wide-eyed, Helen abruptly found herself within the midst of a great mansion. The effect of transitioning from falling down the length of a cliff's facing, to standing upon the marble flooring of an ornate entryway, was deeply jarring, rattling the innermost part of her being. It took her a couple of moments to gain her equilibrium; at least enough to make sense of the things around her.

A curving staircase ran elegantly up the wall to the left, its balustrade fashioned of marble. The stairs connected to the second level where a railed balcony of carved wood afforded an overlook of the foyer. A crystal chandelier of breathtaking magnificence hung from the ceiling directly above her.

At the moment, the building was encompassed by a storm of tremendous magnitude. Lightning flashed violently in the large windows above the entrance and around the doorway, illuminating the huge space and filling the capacious foyer with stark, shadowy forms.

"Oh ... Helen ... welcome," hissed a man's voice when one wave of lightning receded, prompting her to turn swiftly towards the sound.

A man was shuffling towards her from the darkness of a hallway to the left. To her horror, she saw that the back half of his head was gone. He had an ashen look to his skin, and his eyes had the dull glaze of the dead.

His mouth opened again, exposing raw, bleeding gums, and he repeated the unsought greeting, "Welcome, Helen. Welcome ... welcome."

Her eyes narrowing, she found it difficult to accept what her eyes were showing her. She recognized the man as a former member of her staff, a person who had become a severe liability by knowing too much about her financial dealings. His untimely death had been reported to the media as a suicide, but Helen knew the truth of it.

At her command, and away from her sight, the

problem involving the unfortunate staff member had been seen to. In the dark of night, he had received a visit from a state trooper unshakably loyal to Helen. A potential political threat had been eliminated in one blast from a .44 magnum, or so she had thought, until just moments before.

Her mind told her that what she was seeing should have been impossible. The man had been dead for several years, and no person could walk and speak with the entire back half of their head missing.

"Welcome! Helen ... welcome!" another low, breathy voice greeted from behind her.

Looking back and anxiety rising, Helen saw another man emerging from the hallway leading off the other side of the foyer. His head was fully intact, but a large part of his chest cavity was torn out, including the area where his heart should have been.

Once more, an unsettling recognition came to Helen. The man had been another figure from her past whose survival had carried a potential threat to her ambitions. He had been a business partner with her, and the two had made a small fortune in real estate using political leverage provided by Helen.

The transactions became the center of a brief controversy, but the man had proven to be loyal to her. Having taken the fall for Helen and deflecting attention from her, he had willingly gone to prison.

Despite his incarceration and early display of loyalty,

there had still been too much at stake for her to risk having him reconsider his situation someday. Loose ends had to be tied securely, and the man had suffered a heart attack while in prison; though the calamity had not been due to any natural cause.

Visited in his cell during the night by a pair of men sent by Helen, and facilitated by a cooperative prison staff, the slimmest of injections to his back had triggered the fatal heart attack. The place where the needle had been inserted was almost imperceptible, and easily evaded detection in the following autopsy. The cause of death had been declared solidly as being due to natural causes.

Knowing that no man should be able to move with an empty chest cavity, fear rose in Helen. She looked back the other way, and then to the second figure, before eying the marble staircase.

Other maimed figures trudged out of the hallways opening into the grand entryway. Several more appeared along the top of the staircase. Shambling down the steps, they joined the other mangled figures at the bottom.

Helen's dread grew as she recognized all of them, men and women she had arranged to have killed to protect her ascent to power, and the activities she had engaged in. They were the victims of many years of ruthless calculation.

"Welcome, Helen. Welcome ... welcome," the anger-laced chant continued to resonate, rising in volume and filling her ears, despite every effort she made to block it out.

Her hands covering her ears proved entirely useless, and each time she tried to shut her eyes she inexplicably found them open wide once again. Her body forced her to face the gruesome assemblage.

There was no way out from the foyer. Every avenue on the interior was blocked, and she heard the front door opening behind her.

Several more voices coming from outside added to the chant. "Welcome … Helen … welcome."

The figures reached towards her, pressing in from all sides. The thunder outside boomed, and a brilliant flare of lightning revealed the faces of the grisly throng in perfect clarity.

Helen began hyperventilating as she stared into expressions of sheer vengeance, with no way out of the foyer. Opening her mouth, she tried loosing a scream, but no sound would emerge.

***

An instant later, a bright corridor surrounded her, immaculately clean and well-lit. With nerves frayed, Helen sobbed as she stared down the long passageway.

To her astonishment, she could see no end to it. Fearing what she would see behind her, Helen hesitated a moment before she started to turn around.

"Where are you running to, Helen?"

The firm voice caused her to jump back, and her panic to spike. The speaker of the voice proved to be no ghost, nor a hulking monster.

Standing a few paces behind her, at the side of a closed doorway, was a man, around thirty years old and in his physical prime. His clean-shaven face had a youthful luster, but there was nothing soft about his appearance. His squared jaw-line accented a grim expression, and a hard look was entrenched in his dark brown eyes.

His gray t-shirt fit snugly around a broad set of shoulders and finely-sculpted arms. The t-shirt was tucked in at his narrow waist, into a pair of belted black pants that ended in combat boots.

Helen had spent a lifetime around such men. They were the kind who had protected her and done her bidding all throughout her rise to power, from elected state and national offices to her appointment as the Secretary of State.

She took a few breaths, working to regain her composure, and eyed the stoic figure. "Where am I?" she asked him.

A smirk played about the lips of the man, but there was no humor in his eyes. "I do not wish to spoil the thrilling moment when a new arrival comes to realization."

"Realization? What are you talking about?" she asked him, her exasperation mounting fast.

He was the first normal-looking figure she had encountered since her mind had spun awry, and she had found herself on the sprawling desert plain. The brief recollection of the hapless victims being dragged over jagged rocks evoked a momentary shudder.

"It is not for me to tell you, Helen, you must come to the conclusion yourself," the man replied, with an air of patience.

"How do you know my name?" she asked him, a little more sharply. "Who are you?"

"If you want to call me something, you can call me the Soldier," the man replied.

"You didn't answer my other question," Helen pressed. "How do you know my name?"

"A great many people know your name, Helen, and so many were affected by the things you have done," the man replied evenly. "You have touched a great multitude of lives, Helen. Far more than most souls."

The explanation was plausible, as images of her face had been spread far and wide across the span of many years spent in the public spotlight. Video and still images transmitted to millions upon millions propelled her to the heights of notoriety.

Very few women could rival Helen Carville's worldwide fame. Yet while it was likely a person could recognize her, she was not used to the kind of familiarity being expressed by someone who looked to be little more than a common police officer or security guard.

"I don't know you," she said, icily, in an echo of the colder, more aloof demeanor she had so often manifested over the years. "And if you can't tell me why I'm here, then just point me in the direction of someone who can. Then you can go back to tending the doorway."

The smirk came back to the Soldier's lips. "You assume far too much Helen. I am not here because of the doorway. I am here because of you."

"Because of me?" she asked, caught off guard by the response.

"In your case, not only am I here to witness your awakening, but also one of the greatest prominence," the Soldier informed her. "You should consider yourself privileged that one so exalted desired to witness the process of your awakening."

"Who would that be?" she asked, already wondering if she knew who it was that the Soldier was talking about. She had spent a lifetime interacting with the upper crust of power in the world, and was all but certain she would know anyone of prominence or renown.

"You should not think with such limitations," the Soldier replied. "You are in a place where the possibilities far exceed what you were used to. In fact, I think you will find the possibilities inexhaustible, following your awakening."

"You better damn well tell me where I am, who you really are, and what this is all about!" she snapped, frustrated with his enigmatic responses.

"Perhaps a little more personal revelation is in order," he replied calmly.

Before she could give vent to the anger rising inside, he turned and opened the doorway to his left. The light from the corridor did not penetrate the darkness on the other side. Rather, rays of darkness overcame the light, flooding into the corridor and encompassing Helen.

***

Without warning, Helen found herself at the upper edge of a great pit. She gave a start as she peered into the bottom, and found it was filled with writhing forms. Looking closer, her eyes widened, seeing that many of the figures were human, intertwined with misshapen beasts and bizarre, bipedal entities.

Wafting up from the pit, the thick pungency of raw excrement engulfed her, and she gagged violently. Bending over, she clutched at her stomach and heaved, but nothing would come out.

"There is purpose here, Helen," the voice of the Soldier interjected, causing her to straighten back up, despite the nausea wracking her body.

The Soldier was standing at her side, looking down into the pit with a leaden countenance. He did not appear to be bothered in the slightest by the terrible stench or morbid nature of the pit.

"You ... you know what this is?" Helen queried, looking at his face.

"Of course I do," the Soldier replied firmly, continuing

to stare downward. "It is you who needs to come to an understanding."

Following his gaze to the bottom of the pit, she saw a few of the human figures gazing upward. Taking greater note of their condition, she blanched, and the chilly touch of fear ran through her body.

Bleeding, torn wretches, the pitiful figures cried out to her in breathy tones. "Welcome … Helen … Welcome … welcome."

"Who are they?" she asked the Soldier, more plaintively. "What is all of this? What is going on here?"

"Maybe you should go down now, and find out the truth of it all," the Soldier replied, with no trace of emotion, his eyes like glints of steel as he looked over to her.

Before she could reply, her feet began to slide as the edge of the pit crumbled away beneath her. Terror filled Helen as she skidded down the side of the pit, slowly. Unable to stop her descent, she clawed desperately at the muddy surface and tried in vain to dig her heels in.

A bird-headed, long-limbed creature, with freakishly large male genitalia, shrieked as it positioned itself at the bottom of the long descent. Helen slipped further down the slope, drawing closer to the nightmarish thing. Its shrill cries pierced her ears, and she recoiled as she took account of its severe arousal.

In that moment, she began to take in the gruesome frenzy around the bird-creature. The humans were at the mercy of the bestial entities, which were meting out the most brutal savagery. Sickened and horrified at what she saw, her panic and desperation increased as she continued down the face of the slope.

"Oh ... Helen ... Welcome," one of the humans near the bird-thing gasped, an older man whose face she recognized immediately.

He was of her former financial managers, whom she had conducted business with for many years until the day he had died from a natural heart attack. Seeing him, and hearing him speak in this awful place, sent a shock wave through her mind.

A monstrous thing with the general form of a scorpion was pinning him down, such that he could not move a single limb. In place of pincers the horrid entity had six extensive claws at the end of each appendage; curving talons with the length and width of large butcher's knives.

A cold smile came to the old man's face, and he began to laugh hysterically as his tormentor drove all six blade-like claws into the top of his skull. Tears ran down his face as blood oozed from his mouth, nose, and the corners of his eyes.

"Welcome ... Helen," he wheezed, shaking from what could only be a tremendous degree of pain coursing through his body. After a few moments, he added, "It is so good ... to see you again ... Helen."

Helen took her eyes away and screamed, seeing

the bird-creature reaching out for her as she arrived at the bottom of the slope. Its intent filled her mind with merciless explicitness, spiraling her terror upwards and fragmenting her sanity. She flailed and thrashed as the beast lay hold upon her.

***

In a flash, the scene shifted yet again. Instead of a slope, mansion, or pit, she found herself standing in the middle of an empty desert plain.

Breathing fast, she patted her body where the bird-creature had grabbed her, if only to reassure herself that she was truly free of the thing. The air was no longer filled with shrieks and cries, further bolstering the reality that she was no longer within the awful pit.

She realized she was alone. There was no sign of the Soldier, or anything else. For once, being entirely to herself was a tremendous relief.

The hackles on the back of her neck began to rise. Helen had the unwelcome feeling she was being watched, and the momentary comfort she had gained eroded fast.

Gazing around, she saw nothing, just an endless plain of parched, rocky soil. Sulfurous winds swept over her, whistling in her ears.

A feeling of desolation mirroring the starkness of her surroundings filled Helen. She felt so empty and lost, and could not make sense of anything happening to her.

Everything that had happened to her since she had left the roadway and headed into the desert involved something that connected to her life. The ghastly apparitions on the mountainside had the appearances of individuals victimized in military strikes she had supported, facilitated many times, and often celebrated. The maimed figures in the mansion were those whose demises she had personally ordered. The blood-soaked orgy in the pit held a man who had always carried an air of high refinement, during the many years he indulged in luxurious comforts and the trappings of power alongside Helen.

Everything was tied in some way to her. Yet she could still not fathom why it was happening, or what it all implied. Something was eluding her comprehension, and her failure to grasp it was maddening.

Feeling her resolve collapsing inside, she began to cry. The drops from her eyes ran down her cheeks as she stared off into the emptiness of the vast plain.

She could not shake the feeling of being watched. Her head slumped downward, and she saw that the tears falling to the ground were of a crimson hue, even as something deep inside compelled her to bring her eyes upward.

Weeping blood, she gazed into the underbelly of the churning skies. Out of the rolling masses of black ash, a face began to take shape.

To her dismay, Helen realized it was not the face of a

human manifesting above her. Rather, it was something more elongated and angular in its features.

There was elegance to the emerging being's form, but there was also a fearsome aspect to the Entity's appearance. Its eyes pulsed with fire, as it gazed down upon Helen with a decidedly malevolent countenance.

The Entity's voice thundered with a deep resonance, though the texture underlying its tone carried a quality of grating scratchiness. The sound was something alien to Helen, a vocalization that no human being could replicate.

"Welcome to the undying lands," the Entity began. "Every suffering, every sorrow, and every pain you experience will not decrease what you will endure in these realms of dark wonders. The life you led was a glorious tribute to the Master. Now you may claim the reward you chose with the life you lived."

Everything came together at once for Helen, and her mind went dizzy with a flooding delirium of horror and realization. She understood why she had witnessed the things that she had, and everything the Soldier told her now made perfect sense.

She knew precisely where she was, a place of nightmare from which she would never awaken. Even if she begged to die and seek the mercy of oblivion, she knew she could not.

Helen screamed, a terrible cry of the damned, as the enormity of her predicament struck her with savage, merciless force. A realm of horror was now hers forever.

The world she had known was no better than a faded, dead dream, to be entirely forgotten within the shadows of time and space. Terror and hopelessness replaced power and prestige, and would be her trappings, forevermore.

***

Slowly, the Entity withdrew into the black, storm-ridden cloud masses, leaving the haggard and devastated soul alone on the boundless plain. She would not remain unattended for long.

Even then, massive creatures bearing dark chains were lumbering towards her across the arid landscape. Soon, they would be dragging her down a pathway that would initiate her infinite journey through a new state of existence.

A feeling of tremendous satisfaction flowed throughout the Entity's spirit. The moment of the soul's awakening to the infernal realms had been sweeter and more invigorating than the ancient being had imagined.

Her throaty, forlorn scream at her moment of cognizance was cradled within the bosom of the Entity's spirit. It was a delectable sound, a prized possession to be savored, as one of the most powerful among the lords of hell returned to the slumbering depths from which it had roused itself upon her arrival.

BLOOD DREAMS

The malefic Entity crossed many ethereal realms before slipping into the farthest levels of consciousness, gnawing hungers sated again, at least for a period. Any soul torn away from the Source represented an infinite victory in itself; but one who had levied such wickedness and destruction upon the Creator's world was to be cherished profoundly.

There would be time enough to taste the essence of her soul, and indulge in the kind of rapacity that would make the vilest, most wicked of humankind blanch. But for now, it was enough to drift once more upon the currents of a crimson sea; fully embraced within the soothing depths of blood dreams.

THE GROVE

THE GROVE

"It is difficult to free fools from the chains they revere."
-Voltaire

Connor Hillenbrand eased into the soft embrace of the padded leather. Riding in the back seat, he glanced casually out the window as the black Mercedes rolled past the guard checkpoint and continued up the tree-flanked road towards the Grove. The drive to the bevy of cabins, dining hall, and other facilities was always pleasant, engulfing the visitor with a promise of seclusion and haven upon entering the thoroughly-warded locality.

Connor watched the sunlight flickering through the trees lining the road as they meandered through the wooded area. He was already anticipating the repose and frivolity that would be taking place over the next few days. Now in his late seventies, Connor knew there were fewer such visits lying in the future, and he was determined to indulge fully in each and every one he had left.

Oddly, for being a man of such advanced years, Connor felt very youthful at the present moment. It was as if the weight of years had fled him entirely, leaving him with a spry enthusiasm regarding the woodland retreat reserved for men of elite status and privilege.

He welcomed the unexpected feeling of rejuvenation as the car turned a bend and approached a prominent timber structure, serving as both a dining hall and site for hosting larger gatherings during the retreat. The aches of his arthritis were completely absent, and he even felt limber, a very promising omen given the sundry pleasures to be delved into very soon.

The car pulled to a stop. The driver sat in place with the engine idling, as an attendant strode up to the rear door on Connor's side, opening it for him.

"Welcome back to the Grove, Mr. Hillebrand, I trust your ride here was a pleasant one," came the cordial greeting from the sharply-attired young man.

"Very much so. Entering these grounds is like entering another world, one much to my liking," Connor returned politely, getting out of the car and letting his gaze linger for a moment on the handsome face of the dark-haired youth.

Broad shouldered, thin of waist, and graced with unblemished olive skin, the young man was simply exquisite to look upon. He was one Connor would definitely have his sights set on for later, once the libations began flowing, and inhibitions dissipated.

THE GROVE

"Ah, Connor, so glad that you could make it, finally," intoned a deep-toned, familiar voice, coming from the steps leading to the entrance of the grand timber structure.

Connor looked away from the comely youth, as his driver pulled the Mercedes slowly forward. The departing car left a clear path to his longtime friend William Reid, the international banking magnate who had shared numerous visits to the Grove with him.

"What are you inferring … that I 'could make it finally,' " Connor riposted, displaying a wide grin. "I would think I have made it here before half of our little band of world conquering rogues. I know I am in plenty of time for all of our usual little shenanigans, all of which I am really looking forward to. For some reason I feel better than I have in quite some time. It is like I am twenty-five years old again."

William smiled. "Not all have made it here just yet, but eventually everyone you and I know well will be here. You are in time for the Ritual, of course. The sacrifice will be made, as it always has been. But enough of that. Come, let us get a drink, and talk a bit. It has been some time since I have seen you."

Connor strode towards William, taking a deep, relaxing breath, as his mind began settling into the proper mode for the next few days. Wall Street and high volume trading were concerns he could leave far behind, save for sharing a few ideas regarding the course that the powerful in the world would look to be taking in the near future.

Plotting future courses of action was a definite benefit of attending the retreat at the Grove every year. Being among like-minded individuals such as William, all of whom wielded tremendous wealth and influence within the world, Connor was at the vanguard of the trend-setters in the increasingly global climate.

Theirs was the kind of money determining who would be put forth to the public as presidential choices out of primaries, ensuring victory, no matter which party was elected. Any threat to that paradigm was marginalized or scandalized easily enough.

It was Connor's ilk who ultimately wrote a bulk of the yearly legislation, a process involving a legion of well-funded lobbyists ensconced around Washington. The fusion of politics and big money made him laugh every time he heard people decry capitalism in the context of Washington, as what took place in the capital and all around the globe was anything but that kind of system.

While recreation was at the core of the excursion to the Grove, more than a little business could be conducted among men with common interests and concerns. It was not often that Connor found himself among such a large crowd of peers, and like all the others he always took advantage of the occasion.

The little faction of conspiracy theorists regularly protesting the annual event were justified in their claims.

World-affecting decisions were indeed made during the retreat by the sort of men whose vast resources held the kind of power to actuate them. It was anything but a conspiracy; rather, it was simply common sense.

Connor shook William's hand, and the two turned, making their way to the front doors of the grand edifice looming in front of them. "So how have things been, William?" Connor inquired casually, as another attractive young male servant opened the doors for them.

Connor could envision the supple muscle contours underlying the young man's well-tailored dress attire. The thought made his blood rush a little faster.

William cast him a strange expression, and hesitated for a moment. "For the moment, all is well."

"I'm just glad to get away from it all for a few days," Connor replied, as they continued past an array of ornate furnishings, making their way towards a broad marble patio at the rear of the building.

A number of the residential cabins could be seen nestled within the trees beyond the cleared area, which was filled at the moment with a throng of elite individuals. Servants moved amongst them, ferrying trays and interfacing with a few bars set around the perimeter.

"Ahhh ... a nice glass of my favorite red would hit the spot about right now," Connor commented, as they stepped back out into the open air.

"I'm afraid there is no wine, but I bet that they have anything else that you can think of," William replied.

"How unfortunate. I wonder why, that's quite odd, as nothing ever seems lacking here," Connor remarked, looking out over the picturesque scene. The one constant about the Grove; nothing was overlooked when it came to luxuries of drink and cuisine.

The sky was of a light crimson hue, spread solidly above them. Connor gazed upon the strange beauty of it for a moment, as William responded, "I can't really explain that ... it is just the way it is."

Connor hailed one of the servants, who hastened over. The young man took his order for a scotch on the rocks, as he requested a particular type he favored. He turned back to William as the servant headed away to fill his order. "Then a good scotch will have to suffice."

"I'm sure it will be quite fine," William returned.

"So aren't you wondering how I've been doing?" Connor asked him, with a chuckle. "You are not your usual curious self today."

William shrugged noncommittally. "I suppose my mind is not on business at the moment."

"Well, I'll give you the short of it all anyway. Been making a fortune in energy credits. That was one of the best systems that we've ever engineered," Connor boasted, thinking of the piles of revenue he had made in transacting carbon credits over the past year. "Enough trouble getting it firmly in place, but the effort was well worth it, don't you think?"

"I don't think it matters much, not anymore," William

said, an odd timbre to his voice.

Connor's brow furrowed. "Matters much? You are a funny fellow today, William."

William smiled back at him, but said nothing in response. There was something amiss within the look in his eyes.

"Forget about business then, time to have a little fun," Connor said, a little unnerved by his friend's strange behavior. "I'd better make my rounds before the evening gets fully underway."

Begging leave of William, Connor moved among the crowd. He recognized many prominent individuals, though a good number of the usual faces were absent. He wondered about many of those who were not present, having spoken to several quite recently who had indicated they would be attending the Grove as usual.

As the hour passed, the sky above deepened in hue, becoming a darker crimson. Shadows began spreading from the trees to cover the gathering on the patio. Connor always liked the onset of night at the Grove, as darkness shrouded the many indulgences that could be explored.

He knew that many choice individuals were ferried in at great expense to see to the physical desires of the guests. Some of those brought in were quite exceptional specimens, whose prowess had earned them fame in the adult film industry.

The prurient thoughts caused the blood to stir within

his veins, as it would not be much longer before he could immerse in pleasures of a more lustful kind. The Grove was a sanctuary for the powerful attendees, and virtually nothing was off limits within the hedonistic paradise.

First, though, the Ritual would take place, as it did every year at the Grove. With darkness falling, it would not be much longer before summons were issued; for all the attendees to come and bear witness to the sacrifice.

***

Under dark skies and walking in a loose column, the guests made their way along a dirt pathway through the trees. After a modest hike, the pathway ended at the edge of a broad stream. On the opposite side of the water, an impressive display had been erected. It was one Connor and other attendees at the Grove were well familiar with.

Connor had to stifle a chuckle, glancing across at the gigantic owl that had been constructed amongst the pine trees. He always found the idea of a mass of worshippers gathering before a huge owl to be somewhat ridiculous in nature.

A stone altar and concrete trough were set before the owl. It would not be long before hooded figures and a priest, the latter in elaborate vestments and head wear, would be conducting the yearly Ritual.

Like most of the attendees, Connor never took the rite too seriously. The yearly ceremony rooted in grand theatrics, it did nothing more than herald the washing away of all cares while in the Grove.

Rumors abounded that others of Connor's ilk saw it differently, but he did not count himself among them. Yet once one was immersed in the moment, the Ritual and its symbolic sacrifice were intriguing enough to hold a person's attention in a manner resembling a devout adherent of a faith.

He knew what was coming, having witnessed it many times before. An effigy of a human figure would be conveyed across the water, where it would be burned before the great owl in an offering meant to invoke success upon the endeavors of all the attendees during the coming year.

Perhaps there was something to the Ritual, Connor had to admit at times, as it did seem like the regular attendees of the Grove attained greater success with each passing year. Even when the nation was undergoing downturns, his own trajectory had always been on an upward climb, both in influence and wealth.

He attributed his successes to his effort and abilities, but he never forgot the roles that those around him played in creating the kind of world in which a man like him could thrive. In a way, the Ritual represented that reality, and the reaffirmation of that world, even in a strange, ceremonial form with a big owl at the center of it, was a small indulgence of time he could afford.

"His Majesty, great Molec .... " William commented,

looking to Connor as he stood transfixed, gazing across at the sacrificial site and the towering owl. "This Ritual will indeed be a special one for you, Connor. I am very sure of that."

"So the owl has a name this time? Molec you say? Then yes, let us hail great Molec! We'll make the sacrifice, and then we'll get to the real purpose of this place," Connor stated with a wide grin, as salacious thoughts played about the edges of his mind.

"I could not have said it any better," William responded, and there was something about his tone that gave Connor pause.

"I hope you are looking forward to later," Connor said, thinking of the pliant, finely-chiseled bodies he would be caressing and tasting deep into the night.

"Later? Sooner? What does time matter, Connor?" William said, his voice again reflecting a strange undertone. "Time is no concern now."

"I wish you were right and that it would last forever, sometimes," Connor said, thinking of the exquisite pleasures and thrills.

"Oh, it will last forever," William said firmly. "That is another thing I can assure you."

"We can only hope it does," Connor said, though his jest was dampened at the odd demeanor shown by his friend.

Connor glanced about, as darkness deepened across the Grove. He could feel anticipation swirling among the gathered throng, as the atmosphere swiftly took on a magical air. Shadows danced and appeared to come alive right out of the corners of his eyes, prompting him to turn his head and look around more than once.

The night seemed alive, and Connor found his desires surging within. A part of him was beginning feel impatient, and he hoped it would not be much longer before the ceremony got underway. As if his restlessness were some sort of cue, firelight and movements drew his attention.

A procession of torch-bearing, hooded figures strode into sight across the stream, taking up positions all around the stone altar, trough, and enormous owl effigy. A warm breeze wafted through the audience, and Connor wrinkled his nose, catching a thick element of sulfur within it. He much preferred the clean scent of pine in the night air, and wondered what possibly could give off such a pungent stench.

A man garbed in magnificent raiment emerged a moment later, walking slowly to take a position at the foot of the great owl, just behind the stone altar. As Connor had witnessed many times before, the high priest began the ceremony.

Raising his arms, he began to chant in words unintelligible to Connor. Though he had never understood the particular words used in parts of the ceremony, there was something different about the ones he now heard.

A feeling of unease poised to grow inside his gut.

Connor forced it back as best he could. Those conducting the Ritual had probably decided to change things up just a little from the usual. There was no reason for him to have any misgivings about the proceedings.

"I call to all who have gathered to witness ... now, we present the sacrifice to Great Molec," the high priest announced in a resonant voice that carried over the assemblage. "You may bring the sacrifice across ... to please our magnificent lord."

The high priest and all of the shrouded ritual attendants turned and stared in the direction of the group on the other side of the stream. It was yet another anomaly in regards to the ritual Connor had observed so many times before. The unease he had held at bay crept forward inside him.

Connor looked for the boat designated to carry the effigy across the water to be burned before the owl statue. His brow furrowed, as his eyes came to rest upon the small vessel. It was exactly where he expected it to be, but nobody made a move towards it.

Further quickening the discomfiting feelings welling up from within, Connor could see no sign of the effigy. The boat was completely empty.

"What's going on?" Connor whispered to William, needing some kind of answer for the odd differences in the ritual.

"Look around you, Connor," William replied, calmly. "It would seem you have garnered some attention, though not unexpected."

Connor turned his head slowly, a chill creeping up his spine as he recognized all the attendees around him looking squarely in his direction. A number of them were grinning at him, though none of the icy expressions held any sign of affinity. A nerve-wracking silence had fallen over the entire grove.

A prickly feeling crawled along Connor's skin, as the crowd began parting. Four figures in long white robes and hoods approached him. He made no move to avoid them, incredulous that their attentions were oriented upon him.

"Where's the offering?" Connor stammered, unable to contain his silence any longer.

"The offering?" a man near him stated, with a throaty chuckle. "Why don't you tell him, William? You know him well enough. And there's no harm in doing so now. I would say he is going to find out anyway."

William nodded, and turned slowly towards Connor. "Connor, don't you realize what is happening? The offering is right here," he stated.

A smile spread across his face, an expression as cold as the laughter breaking out of him a moment later. Something took hold of William that Connor had never experienced before.

The calm, collected look of a banking magnate was entirely absent. Connor's friend now had the manic look of a consummate madman, his face contorting into something devoid of reason and sanity.

"Oh Connor, you should see your face now," William continued, almost chortling in a mockery of merriment. "The offering, my friend, is you, Connor! It is your grand welcome to a new existence!"

His friend's words stabbed into his consciousness, paralyzing Connor as his mind spun trying to grasp everything swirling inside his head. It was as if he was waking up inside of a very bad dream, but he did not know how he could get out of it.

The throng began chanting rhythmically in the strange language the high priest had first used, as a pair of the white-robed figures stepped forward and seized Connor with iron-strong grips. For a moment he tried tussling with the figures apprehending him, but they nearly wrenched his arms out of his sockets, half-dragging, half-carrying him to the boat lodged on the near shore.

Forcing Connor down into the boat, the robed figures joined him inside it. Staring across the water, a couple of his escorts took up paddles. The others kept their grip fixed upon him, digging long nails into his skin that made their fingers seem like claws. His mind was racing, struggling to comprehend the sharp turn of events that had just occurred.

Only moments before he had been savoring thoughts of shacking up in one of the bungalows with one, if not two, of the beautiful young men the Grove gave him access to. Now he was being ferried across the stream against his will, moments after seeing his longtime friend take on the countenance of a raving lunatic. Nothing made sense, and everything was transpiring all too fast.

The boat came to rest on the farther shore, and Connor found himself yanked out of the boat. Connor struggled in vain against the hooded figures as they lugged him up from the shore towards the stone altar and trough. Bearing him forcibly down into the trough, binding his limbs such that he was rendered entirely immobile, the quartet of figures remained in place as the priest joined them for the resumption of the ceremony.

Connor recoiled in terror as his eyes took in the putrescent figure garbed in the vestment and headdress. Rotted flesh, speckled with pus-oozing sores, covered the priest.

His eyes were hollow sockets, pools of darkness holding no flicker of life within them. The hideous being's lips had been ripped away completely, leaving his mouth in an incessant, mirthless smile comprised of jagged teeth and bloodied gums.

Glancing about, panic soared within Connor as he saw what lay underneath the hoods of the figures that had conveyed him across the stream. Elongated serpentine heads, crowned by spiky ridges, tilted down towards him. The reptilian visages harbored gazes filled with malevolence, or perhaps the look of a constrictor gazing upon a cornered rat.

Connor pulled his gaze away from the frightening, inhuman countenances, and stared up at the great owl. Instantly, a spike of icy terror lanced through him.

The surface of the statue was shimmering, and something alive and sentient appeared to be manifesting. The image of the owl statue dissipated steadily, and it looked as if the entire construct was coming to life.

Blazing eyes gazed down upon Connor, as vast onyx wings, six in number, spread from behind the towering figure's back. No longer an effigy, a being ancient, strong, and proud loomed enormously over Connor.

At first, the face of the entity was something of stunning beauty. Neither male nor female, but instead a harmony of androgyny, the enrapturing visage captivated Connor for just a moment.

Then the mouth of the being began to spread wider, altering the balance of its features as a host of serrated teeth came into view. There was nothing comely about the monstrous appearance emerging to drown out the entity's initial appearance.

Connor strained to move within the trough, as he began to shake and whimper uncontrollably. Sweat streamed in rivulets to each side of his face, and his bowels felt as if they had turned to water. The terror he felt was beyond delirium.

The chants from the attendees were growing louder, and the menacing titan looming over him filled all of his vision. He had never felt more helpless, or experienced the complete absence of hope that pervaded him now.

As the chanting reached a feverish crescendo, flames erupted from within Connor, and raced to cover his entire body. He writhed and tried to scream, though no sound emerged as an indescribable agony engulfed him. Consumed with horrific pain, Connor barely took notice of the massive hands of Molec as the huge being reached down into the trough and picked up his burning body.

Connor was helpless as he was brought closer to the cavernous maw of the demonic entity. There was no escaping his plight, and though he was awash with terror the mercy of unconsciousness cruelly evaded him.

He somehow managed to force his eyes away, catching a glimpse of the area on the opposite side of the stream. Where William and the others had been assembled in good order was now a raging scene of chaos. Dark, shadowy forms scuttled among the attendees, as shrill cries of pain and maddened laughter filled the air.

An orgy was getting underway, though in no way was it a pursuit of sexual pleasures. Rather, it was a feast of violence, as William and the other attendees were being ripped apart and consumed by their monstrous tormentors. High-pitched shrieks of agony erupted everywhere, joined by the guttural roars of the dark entities roving amongst the crowd.

A deeper understanding entered Connor's mind as he gazed upon the futile struggles of the humans against the ravenous shadow-beasts. Trappings of privilege and status were nowhere to be found, and no mercy would be shown.

The darkness Connor's friends and colleagues had engendered over the long years of their life was now alive, manifested fully with them in the Grove. They had created the darkness, and it had patiently awaited them in many diverse forms. It would await others who trod a path of power and prestige that led to ultimate desolation.

Connor could only imagine what kinds of monsters had been given life by his own actions. His eyes rolled upward, staring into the fiery maw of Molec as the demonic titan took the entirety of his body into its gaping jaws.

As Connor tumbled into the dark, fathomless depths within the gorge of Molec, Connor realized with full clarity that he had died peacefully in his sleep, just prior to his arrival at the Grove. His burning body was consumed savagely, shredded into countless pieces within Molec. He felt each and every piece of his soul being eviscerated, all the while knowing this was just the start of an unending nightmare.

One distant speck of his conscious awareness realized he would not be given the mercy of oblivion, and that the darkness he had given life to would be revealed to him. Another faint part of him knew he would be joining William again soon; as a group of men who held tremendous wealth and power in another life gathered to welcome another soul's arrival to the Grove.

THE SMALLEST FISH

THE SMALLEST FISH

"Adversity makes men, and prosperity makes monsters."
-Victor Hugo

"Where in the hell am I?" the man murmured, his voice barely above a whisper.

He stared out across the silent cityscape. If not for the fact that all his physical senses felt heightened, vibrant and far beyond anything he had ever felt before in his life, Carlos would have attributed the whole experience to nothing more than a sequence within a very strange dream.

Past physical aspects such as vivid sight and exceptional hearing, a thick fog of confusion reigned deeper inside his head. He knew without a doubt he did not have full possession of his mental bearings. For a man so used to having a sharp, decisive wit, and maintaining a clear state of awareness, the feeling was incredibly disconcerting; and highly unwelcome.

Something farther inside told Carlos that his skin should not be so smooth, nor should his muscles be in as supple and shapely a state as they now were. He had the vague impression that he should have possessed a considerably older body, something closer to fifty-five than thirty. The discordant notion tugged forcibly at the edges of his hazy conscious awareness.

Yet he was not about to argue with his current physical state. Youthful, vital, and full of vigor, he felt entirely wonderful. Whatever he might have otherwise been, he was now at the apex of his physical prime.

Even so, the keen edges to his senses were not entirely beneficial. The air was dense, almost stifling, and decidedly hot. The breezes and gusts of wind he felt coursing over his body brought no sense of relief. In truth, they were even hotter than the still air, and carried a faint, sulfurous scent along the tendrils of their currents.

Carlos wrinkled his nose in disgust as one particularly pungent wave flowed over him. He gagged and teetered on the cusp of vomiting.

Turning away from the noxious wind, he gazed in the other direction, peering down the lengthy city avenue. The nauseating feeling ebbed at last, but something was undeniably wrong with the scene spread out before him. Of that he was certain, even if he could not yet clear the lingering daze from his head.

Everywhere he looked, Carlos realized he was alone. What cars could be seen looked as if they had been burned and abandoned long ago; skeletal husks strewn randomly down the length of the wide boulevard.

Traffic lights at the intersections all the way down the thoroughfare, as far as his eyes could see, remained frozen on red. The lights flickered off and on, as if barely sustained by the electric grid powering them.

The cars were not the only unsightly elements. Trash piles and a variety of other debris littered the street and sidewalks copiously, giving the sense that the streets had been left unattended for a very long time.

Something was truly amiss with the city itself. A foreboding aura permeated the scene, infusing Carlos with a deep sense of unease.

Carlos slowly tilted his head from the street upward, looking towards the tops of the buildings lining the hushed thoroughfare. His eyes narrowed, as he took in the jagged summits of the surrounding structures.

Like broken teeth set against a crimson sky, the buildings, decaying and crumbling, were all in a terrible state of upkeep. Less than a handful of windows had been left intact along the rise of their towering facades.

Carlos shook his head, entirely bewildered, and slowly stepped forward along the crack-ridden pavement. The street was most certainly 10th Avenue in the city he had lived in for many years, enjoying a life of comfort and luxury that so few ever attained. In fact, one of the high rises in his immediate field of view, farther down the street to the right side, held his opulent office suites that were the envy of many of the city's business elite.

A rising hope that familiarity would bring a better cognizance of what was going on compelled him towards the structure. Carlos shuffled down the street, suddenly feeling more than a little lethargic as he made his way towards the entrance to the edifice. The soles of his shiny black dress shoes scratched against the dry pavement, creating the only sounds other than the winds whistling through the channels between the seemingly abandoned buildings.

Once an elegant line of glass doors and windows, with a large, revolving door set at the center, the entryway to the lofty office building was easy enough to access. Glass lay all about the area, in an abundance of shards and fragments strewn all around, and there were no impediments to going inside. Carlos stepped carefully, relieved that he had on a pair of leather wingtip shoes, which cost as much as some individuals made in an entire month of working.

Scanning the capacious entry chamber, Carlos' brow furrowed deeper as he took in the empty guard station. Normally, two or three uniformed security guards held court at the circular counter, a watchful island within the grand atrium. The guards, aided by the bevy of surveillance monitors arrayed beneath the counter top, kept a vigilant eye on those seeking access to the offices above. At the moment, anyone could come and go, and there was no respectful, deferential greeting to meet

Carlos' own entry.

Just beyond the guard station was a short hallway, flanked on either side by three elevators. The six shafts comprised the core access to the executive suites on the levels above.

As was the case out on 10th Avenue, there were still signs of working electricity. Lights flickered off and on as Carlos walked slowly past the guard station and continued towards the elevators. He chose the first set of doors to the right.

Carlos pressed the up button and waited until the door finally opened with a disconcerting creaking that belied the silent, flawlessly smooth operation he had always observed before. He stepped into the shadowy carriage, turning aside and hitting the button for the sixteenth floor, almost as an afterthought. The doors closed slowly, emitting the same, troubling sound of internal instability.

A frown crossed his face, and his stomach tightened, as the carriage abruptly lurched upward, rattling and shaking along its ascendant path. Carlos had always taken for granted how the carriage would glide so gracefully up the long shaft, providing him express access to his office suites.

The carriage came to a sudden halt, causing Carlos to stagger and his heart to sharply pick up a few beats. The doors shuddered as they spread apart, revealing the broad, semicircular reception desk with the prominent

Adept Industries International logo looming behind it.

The edge that had been building within Carlos ebbed a little as he set his eyes upon Mari, the gorgeous blonde who had been employed for several years as his principle receptionist. She was sitting at her post as he had always remembered, hair and makeup immaculately fixed.

"Good ... morning, Mr. Chavez," she greeted with a smile, flashing her perfectly white teeth, all even and immaculate in appearance.

Carlos immediately caught her hesitation, as if she had to suddenly think for a moment about what time of day it was. Behind the comely smile, he could also sense an unmistakable nervousness. Her eyes betrayed a deeper unease, of a kind that even her beautiful outward appearance was unable to mask.

"I hope that it's a good day. Everything seems a little strange this morning, for some reason," Carlos replied casually.

"Most of us have been waiting for you," she responded evenly.

The answer was decidedly strange, as Carlos was always prompt in arriving to the office each day and every day as he applied himself to growing and maintaining his prodigious financial empire. Further, it was clear that the day was far from being well underway. No phones rang, and there was none of the usual bustle about the area. Only Mari and Carlos stood at the entrance to the office suites.

THE SMALLEST FISH

"Well, I definitely don't make it a practice to keep any of you waiting," Carlos said, with a slight hint of irritation.

"It has been a long time ... for a few of us," Mari replied, in a lower tone of voice.

"Whatever the case may be, I need to find some things out. I'm not feeling my best at the moment and could use your help. Why don't you walk with me for a moment," Carlos said, trying to digest her odd words, and suddenly feeling a compelling desire to keep someone with him.

Nodding, she stood up, and walked around the back of the broad reception desk to join him at its front. Dressed in a form-fitting white blouse, tantalizingly high mini-skirt, and black high heels, her attire favorably accented her shapely figure.

Carlos eyed the contours of the toned muscles flowing along her long, exquisite legs, the alluring sight evoking a little dryness in his throat. His eyes roved a little higher, and he felt his blood pick up in pace as he eyed another prominent, curvaceous portion of her body.

She was as skillful as she was attractive, magnifying the effect even more. Carlos had experienced her considerable sensual abilities on more than one occasion, and the sweaty, thrilling escapades had never interfered with their work relationship.

As much as he would have liked to scrutinize her exquisite female form for a little longer, Carlos needed some answers soon. Pursuits of a more carnal nature would have to wait until later. Walking past her, he led Mari off down the hallway to the left.

Reaching his office, a glance inside stalled his thoughts. Behind a broad, semicircular desk, the towering fish tank that had been his pride and joy stood no more. Jagged shards and shattered glass the only echo of the magnificent display, Carlos lamented the loss of a prized possession.

It had been a predator tank, holding several types of fish that occupied varying levels of the tank. Carlos had spent hours upon end over the years savoring the feeding sessions, in which throngs of small fish were loosed at once into the tank, all to their eventual doom.

Some snapped up just beneath the surface, others swallowed midway down, and still others consumed at the bottom, a few always escaped the predators' initial, frenzied onslaught. The survivors intrigued Carlos the most, trapped in a tank with no escape or hope of intervention.

No matter where they strayed, one of the predators eventually caught up to them. The inevitability of the smaller fish's fate gave Carlos a rush that he likened to the times he crushed opposition to his business projects.

Now, Carlos would be bereft of the electrifying thrill provided by that tank, not to mention the expensive fish he maintained in there. It angered him that such a mess had been left in his office, adding to the surreal nature of the environment. He had to get some answers soon.

With quickened strides, he headed towards the door of one of his high-powered attorneys, a man named Darius Jackson. Darius was the lion among his core of stalwart attorneys, tough-spirited and aggressive. If anyone could help Carlos gain a handle on what was going on, the elite lawyer certainly stood as his best option.

The entrance to Darius' office was wide open as Carlos approached. In fact, the door was entirely off its hinges, and lying out in the hallway. A chilling sense of unease crept into Carlos, as he recognized that the door had been violently ripped off the hinges. Gouges with jagged shards marked the places in the frame where the hinges had once been affixed.

Carlos had to step onto the prone mahogany door in order to access the attorney's office. Things were certainly getting stranger with every passing moment, a course of development that Carlos did not like at all.

Darius paced back and forth within his office, in front of what would have been floor to ceiling windows, if the glass had still been in place.

The hot, discomfiting breeze that Carlos had felt down on the street poured into the office space, tossing loose papers about and bathing him in its sweltering heat upon his entrance. In mere moments, the streams of stifling currents brought beads of sweat percolating onto his forehead, which soon turned into thin rivulets trekking down his cheeks and neck.

"Hahahaha!" Darius laughed boisterously, looking

up towards Carlos and Mari as they entered. He threw his head back, looking upward and grinning broadly, before lowering his gaze and shaking his head emphatically. He burst out with another round of robust laughter.

His eyes were wide, and he looked very animated, more like the man he was at lavish parties at night, rather than the composed, steely figure he was during the business day. The cuffs on his off-white shirt were rolled up, and his collar hung open, devoid of the immaculate tie that normally occupied that territory. Dark spots of sweat showed prominently on his shirt, soaking through the fabric around his armpits and upper chest.

"They cheated me ... wait til' I get a hold of them!" Darius exclaimed rabidly. "You just wait! I'll handle it my way! Dammit, I will handle it my way!"

He slammed his fist into his palm, and then gestured forcefully towards the surface of his large oaken desk. Upon it sat a little metallic tray, with a few streaks of white powder. From their current arrangement, Carlos could tell there had been a few more lines upon the tray very recently.

The sight caught Carlos off-guard, and at first he was speechless. Darius normally kept his work and his play well separated. The blurring of the two worlds was yet another bizarre occurrence within a day that was going more off-kilter by the moment.

"Nothing. Not a damned thing. Garbage!" raged Darius, his face contorting through several angry expressions. "And I'm sick of this hot weather. Damned sick of it! Always this heat! Always! Always this damned stench! It never lets up!"

Carlos had to admit that the weather was anything but enjoyable. The skies held a deep, reddish hue, looking eerily blood-red in his estimation. Smoky tendrils scudded across the skies, and he could not see any sign of the sun from his current vantage. The former would have passed for clouds, but they moved much faster than any clouds Carlos ever remembered. He did not dwell long on the unsettling sight, not wanting to take any further notice of unprecedented differences.

Darius' head then turned towards Carlos, as if he had only just become aware of his presence.

"Everyone's been waiting for you, man. So nice of you to finally join us. Very considerate of you, Carlos! Some of us have gone out to take a look around. Would you look at the city? What the hell is wrong with it?" Darius asked, his words flowing quickly, an edginess readily apparent in his voice.

"That's the very question I have today, but we aren't going to learn anything by standing around here," Carlos remarked evenly.

"Then why don't we go down to take a look at the new building site," Darius said, still talking quickly. "I know a few from the office had headed down that way, after waiting here quite a while for you to get here. Can't blame them, you sure took your time, man!"

"Hey!   Drop the accusatory tone, now!" Carlos snapped at Darius, unaccustomed to being addressed by one of his firm's top lieutenants in such an abrasive way.

"Sorry man ... sorry," Darius said in a placating fashion, holding his hands up. The look on his face lost the lively, slightly crazed ambiance it had moments before, as if he had abruptly been thrust back into his normal demeanor. He added apologetically, in a lower voice. "Just been here awhile, that's all."

"Awhile? None of you could have been waiting more than an hour or so. It's still morning, and there sure as hell isn't anything going on here," Carlos growled.

Darius looked about to respond, but suddenly tensed, and held back whatever words had come to his lips. To Carlos' eyes, it appeared that his top lawyer was harboring something of great importance that he did not want to tell him. Even worse, Carlos got the sense that whatever information Darius was restraining was being kept back for his own benefit.

***

Carlos, Darius, and Mari walked towards the high fence serving as the boundary line for the construction site's outer perimeter. Looking in at the masses of rubble contained within it, a hot flash of irritation rose up within Carlos.

He had thought construction had been proceeding

well enough on the site. The last reports he had read indicated the skeleton of several stories had been set in place, and would soon begin to be fleshed out.

Not one thing had been built in the disarrayed space before him. Even the deep pit for the building's lower foundation was completely filled with masses of rubble. Strangely, the signs displaying construction information looked rusted and aged, as if they had been hanging there for years.

"Carlos! Hey, there you are, finally!"

Carlos looked off to the right, and saw Jacob Schwartz approaching. He was the resourceful city councilman who had done such a masterful job of invoking eminent domain to Carlos' advantage.

He had gotten rid of the veritable shacks that had previously stood there, as well as the penniless losers who had occupied them. Many of the previous occupants had lived there for years, some for decades. Their very presence wasted a prime piece of city real estate. At least that was before Carlos thought of turning the real estate plot into a complex of shops and premium apartments. It was an extensive development project that promised steady tax revenue, and an immediate elimination of the decades-old eyesore.

Carlos had been very amused at the feeble attempts to block the eminent domain movement. With politicians, officials, business leaders, and money overwhelmingly on his side, Carlos endured the harmless criticism hurled his way by impotent activists, and put down all resistance without breaking a sweat. He was not interested in popularity contests, only the advancement of his own agenda.

Of course, he had often laughed and jested with his lawyers and project managers about ridding the area of the rats that had been infesting the area for far too long. The reference was not entirely exaggerated, for that was precisely what the previous occupiers were in Carlos' eyes: a teeming mass of dirty, diseased, scuttling rats.

Jacob looked more than a little disheveled, his short brown locks out of place, and a several-days stubble of growth on his usually clean-shaven face. His light blue shirt and gray pants were sweat-stained and severely wrinkled, both in sore need of a good pressing. His appearance closely mirrored Darius', in that both were very anomalous from their usual states.

"What the hell is going on here?" Carlos queried with a trace of exasperation, having never seen Jacob in this kind of disorderly condition before.

Before Jacob could respond, the project manager of the development, a heavy-set man named Benton Davison, came trudging into sight. He was already within the confines of the construction area, walking into view around a tall mound of debris at least a couple of stories high.

"Benton! What is all this?" Carlos shouted heatedly to the heavy-set man through the fence. He was rapidly losing patience with the continuing lack of answers, not to mention the utterly weird behavior of those around him. ""What is going on here? I demand some answers now!"

Benton looked towards Carlos, but did not respond. He continued hustling towards a nearby entryway, which allowed passage through the high fence line warding the site.

There was a sense of great urgency to his movements. Very conspicuously, he kept looking back over his shoulder, as if expecting to see something behind him at any moment.

"Answer me, now!" Carlos snapped at him. "Damn you, Benton! What is going on here?"

He then noticed there was a big padlock on the chain link doorway Benton headed towards. Out of patience, Carlos strode over and grasped the padlock. Clicking the bolts into place, he firmly secured the doorway and prevented Benton from entertaining any easy notion of exit.

Benton's eyes widened with fright as soon as he saw what Carlos had done. In reality, it was a look that went much farther beyond fright, to something more like sheer terror. He watched Benton begin to tremble, wondering why the man was having such a dramatic reaction to such a menial action.

"That's right, you aren't getting out of there until you start giving me some answers. This big charade ends here, with you, right now! What have you been doing here? And why is the site in such a disastrous mess?" Carlos challenged him. His tone then took on a mocking edge, fueled by his anger. "What? Did the rats come back to try to regain their hovels again? Is it the rats again, Benton? Wanting their dilapidated huts? You can't handle a few rats, Benton?"

Carlos chuckled, as he thought of the powerless miscreants he had swept out from the plot. Their efforts to resist him had been perfect fodder for the periodic amusements of Carlos and those around him.

"No ... Nooooo!" Benton stammered, suddenly looking over his shoulder, paying no attention to Carlos' berating.

Movements out of the corner of his eye drew Carlos' own attention past Benton, towards the top of some of the rubble-mounds. Creeping up and over, with elongated snouts, were several of the largest rats Carlos had ever witnessed. The creatures were each around fifty pounds, at the very least, easily matching the size of a medium-sized dog in girth and length.

The eyes of the macabre rodents appeared to glow, unless the strange effect was just a trick of the light. Saliva dripped profusely from their jaws, which were freakishly long in proportion to their bodies. Outside of the most imaginative movies and video games Carlos had never seen garish creatures like these in all of his life.

"What ... the hell?" Carlos managed to utter, the

words coming forth like a whisper, as incredulity gripped him tightly. The sight challenged all senses of reality, even more so than the dilapidated condition of the city.

Benton cried out in frenzied terror, as several of the eerie creatures began scrabbling down the mounds and hurrying steadily towards him. Carlos willed himself to focus on the situation at hand, and looked back towards the padlock. It then struck him that in his impulsiveness he had not stopped to consider whether or not he or Benton had a key handy.

"Who's got a key to this lock? Jacob? Darius?" Carlos asked quickly, looking back to the others.

A pit formed in his stomach as they all shook their heads from side to side. Darius and Jacob stared towards the phantasms within the fence-line, seemingly transfixed. Mari was looking away, tears starting to flow abundantly down her face, streaking her make-up. Oddly, none of the three seemed to be as shocked about the macabre situation as Carlos was.

"Nobody? You've got to be kidding me! What's going on here?" Carlos responded quickly, looking back into the construction site. "What are those things?"

Carlos' companions remained silent observers, offering no response to his questions. There was nothing that could be done now but watch, as more and more of the hideous, rodent-like creatures emerged into view.

Benton finally reached the fence line. He clutched frantically onto the metal links and whimpered pitifully, even as the air behind him filled with a spine-chilling chorus of chitterings, screeches, and bizarre sounds resembling low-pitched hisses.

"Hahahahahaha!"

The spirited laughter erupted from just to Carlos' left, harboring a maniacal edge that erased any notions of good humor within the sound. A tall man was standing a short distance to Carlos' right. A broad-brimmed hat sheltered his face, and a long, flowing duster of the same hue disguised his bodily features.

"Did well by your friends, didn't you? Oh, you did really well by them, for sure," the Stranger addressed Carlos. "Glad you finally could join them. They've been waiting, I can assure you ... some for quite awhile. It almost isn't fair that it took you so long to get here. But you are here now, and that's what matters."

"Who the hell are you?" Carlos shot back to the Stranger, before looking back to see what had become of Benton's plight.

At least two dozen of the rat-creatures were now bearing down on the hapless man, as he made a futile effort to climb the tall chain-link fence. The heavy-set man could not even get the tips of his shoes into the links, nor could he heft his considerable girth.

"He'll be back, don't worry yourself for a minute!" the Stranger said, in a mockery of reassurance that was accompanied by a wry grin. "Once he's experienced the joys of a full decomposition, that is ... most likely in several parts, from the looks of things. It is a very thorough experience, I am sure. Not one I'd really like though. Maybe ask him about it later. You locked him in there, you realize. I'm sure he'll be happy to talk to you when he comes back."

Carlos' mind swirled, having no idea of what the Stranger was talking about. The man seemed even crazier than his companions.

The rat-like creatures had fanned out wider as they approached, creating a semi-circle and cutting off all hope of escape for Benton. Once the periphery was formed, they closed the semicircle tighter and tighter as they began to converge towards their intended victim.

Benton's wails filled the air, desperate and charged with naked fear. "God, oh god, oh god, oh god," he managed to stammer, blubbering as he alternated between looking back at the monstrous rodents, and clawing uselessly at the fencing.

"Can you help him?" Carlos implored the Stranger.

"Nope ... the rats around here can't be gotten rid of so easily, I'm afraid. This is their home, and he's the trespasser," retorted The Stranger sharply, and Carlos had the feeling there was a biting accusation laced within the words. The Stranger glanced upward, a flicker of recognition in the man's eye. "Your friend, and those things, are the least of your worries, my friend."

Benton screamed behind Carlos, kicking and punching at the huge rat-beasts as the first two of the slavering throng lunged at him. His cries turned to agony as their sharp claws and spiky teeth began to shred his body apart. One bit off half of his face with just a single bite, shearing his nose right off, while another left his right arm as a mangled stub, devoid of wrist and hand.

Carlos watched the terrible slaughter in a surreal state of shock, as if time itself stood still for him to witness the fullness of the horrific scene. Many more of the hideous creatures rushed in, joining in the grisly repast. Within mere moments, Benton was reduced to so much bloodied, pulped flesh. Carlos' stomach churned as he listened to the sickening crunches of Benton's bones being ground into nothing.

Snapping his head back around, Carlos looked about for the Stranger. A loud, piercing shriek suddenly cleaved the air.

Something very large swooped by in a blur, far too fast to follow with the eye. Jacob's screams echoed in the streets a moment later, imbued with a mixture of great desperation and fear, not unlike the cries Benton had just made.

Carlos only caught a brief glimpse of something very long and skeletal, with a leathery, thin layer of skin that had a very desiccated appearance to it. The flying entity had substantially broad wings, and a head that was anything but human, or even bird-like, in form.

Jacob was helpless, born aloft by the malformed being, his body heavily skewered by the creature's hooklike talons. The creature flew around the corner of one of the buildings, taking Jacob along with it. The poor man's cries continued to reach Carlos' ears, though fading in volume as he was born away into the depths of the city.

The high-pitched laughter rang out again, shrill and maniacal. "Oh, I should have warned you about them. Not good for that poor fellow. Not good at all. Sign of things to come, my friend ... welcome to a world of wonders! Oh, it has just begun for you, hasn't' it? Excited yet?" the Stranger queried cheerily, as he came back into sight from where he had evidently taken cover, by one of the car husks in the near vicinity.

The Stranger looked skyward again, a grim smile splayed across his face. "We'd better get a move on it. Plus, you don't want to miss what's heading this way. No, you don't want to miss what's coming right this way, not for a moment. You are in for some amazing things. You like action? I know you do, Carlos! Well, get ready to feel the thrill! We are just getting warmed up. And oh, how hot it can get in here ... how hot it can get."

He laughed again, and Carlos could not shake the impression that the man was gripped by insanity. Even so, he would rather take his chances with a man who seemed to have some understanding of the environment, especially with things like the flying nightmare and the ghastly rat-beasts abounding in the city.

How everything had come to this state would have to wait until a later time. Still frustrated in his desire for answers, Carlos had to believe they would be forthcoming at some point.

***

Keeping tucked to the sides of buildings, so they were not left too exposed out in the open, the Stranger led Carlos, Darius, and Mari on a long hike through the empty streets. He guided them to a building of modest height, set near the outskirts of the decaying city.

Carlos had no idea how much time had passed. He found to his chagrin that it was very difficult for him to even gain a sense of time. What should have been like a moment, felt like an age, and what appeared to be lengthy, seemed like an instant. Any attempt to get a firmer hold on the matter proved to be an exercise in the ephemeral and elusive. In a way, it was like being in the depths of a dream, albeit one imbued with full lucidity.

Similarly, he could not ascertain how far the little party had traveled. It was like his mind could not focus completely, and was riddled with subtle disconnects. Carlos finally resigned himself to the simple task of keeping pace with the Stranger, all the while keeping a constant eye upon the skies.

Like all the other buildings Carlos had encountered, the one that the Stranger guided them to was entirely abandoned. Finding a stairwell just inside the entrance, the group ascended several flights of steps.

THE SMALLEST FISH

After climbing a final short flight of steps, they passed through a door and reemerged back into open air, standing on the uppermost heights of the building. Behind them, a brick outbuilding encased the stairwell, while the edge of the roof was a few paces away.

Poking just above that boundary was the top of a ladder connecting down to an iron platform bound by thin railing. The latter served as the top of a rust-riddled fire escape that ran down the side of the edifice.

Carlos peered outward, in a state of utter shock. Beyond the edge of the city was a vast desert plain. The barren wasteland spread out to the horizons, with nothing to break the desolate continuum.

"Oh, that's not so good," quipped The Stranger, standing at Carlos's right side, gazing downward.

Carlos followed the Stranger's eyes, and saw a few places below on the street level where pockets of people had gathered. Aside from those in his own party, they were the first people Carlos had seen since he had taken in his initial sights of the unsettling, dilapidated city.

"You look a little surprised. What, did you think this entire show was all for you?" the Stranger asked him with a grin, chuckling as he shook his head. "What a confident man you are! I like that kind of hubris, even if it won't get you very far around here."

"I don't know what to think right now," Carlos snarled, becoming increasingly irritated with the Stranger's flippant attitude.

"You'll find out soon enough. No avoiding that. Maybe you'll survive. Then, you can just survive it all again …. And again … and again and again … and again and again and again and … "

Manic laughter ringing out, the Stranger's body shook within the throes of his effusive display. Carlos looked straight into the man's eyes, and held no further doubts that the Stranger was indeed ensnared in the clutches of sheer insanity. His eyes veritably sparkled, their surfaces shining with a crazed gleam.

Carlos did not look at The Stranger for very long, as a faint howling sound reached his ears from the far distance. Though low in volume, the noise made his blood run cold.

The Stranger's laughter broke out again. "Here they come! Oh yeah, get ready for the big show, boys and girls! Oh, this is going to be a good one, if you like things of an epic scale," the Stranger pronounced. He then gestured towards the small groups of people milling about the lower streets, visible clearly from the high vantage. "Oh those folks down there are going to have a lot of fun … sure are going to get far more than they ever bargained for! I can guarantee it. And you too! Don't feel left out, boys and girls! Begin the begin! Let's get it on! It's showtime!" The Stranger chortled merrily, watching the people below.

A pit formed in Carlos' stomach, noticing that the eerie howling was slowly, and steadily, rising in volume.

THE SMALLEST FISH

The swelling, sepulchral cacophony pulled his attention back towards the desert plain. Barely - just barely - he could make out a solid line on the farthest edge of the horizon.

"What ... the hell ... is that?" Darius asked in a tense voice, from where he stood at Carlos' left.

"You'll see soon enough. Don't want to spoil the big surprises for you all!" The Stranger exclaimed, displaying a giddy demeanor. "Not too much longer. Takes a little time to cross that much ground, but you'll see! No worries! No worries at all! Time, ha! Now there's an obsolete concept! Patience, patience, my new friend. Welcome to a world of dark wonders! A place where all things are possible, and there's always a thrill! A place that lasts ... and lasts ... and lasts!" Crazed laughter burst from within him.

"What the hell is wrong with you, man? You are completely psychotic!" Darius shot back, his eyes narrowing in anger.

"I've survived every wave I've seen! Every one of them! Best you listen, my friend, and listen really good," the Stranger retorted, snippets of laughter intertwining with his words. A triumphant look beamed from the depths of the madness holding court in his eyes. "Will you listen? Will you survive? We'll find out! You either will, or you will not! Simple enough for you? Only two outcomes! No more, no less!"

A deep-seated dread began welling up within Carlos,

as the ghastly howling continued rising in volume. He could now see that the dark line was gradually drawing nearer to the outskirts of the city, completely blanketing the ruddy surface of the desert behind it. He began to pick out some distinctive elements within the dissonance, such as high shrieks and grating screams.

Looking back down, he could see that the groups of people scattered among the lower buildings on the city outskirts were taking full notice of the swelling noise. They looked extremely nervous, some maneuvering about to try to see what was causing the commotion, while others moved to take up various kinds of hiding places.

"Always what comes next … such a simple rule … oh so simple…. What comes next... What comes next... What comes next... What comes next! " The Stranger said, getting more animated as he repeated the three word phrase faster and faster. Turning suddenly, he walked over and slammed his forehead against the brick of the outbuilding behind him, drawing blood from the repetitive blows. "What comes next... What comes next... What comes next!"

The Stranger paused, looked back at Carlos, and smiled wide, bearing the most crazed expression he had ever witnessed on a human face. Then the Stranger struck his head flush several more times on the brick surface, blood spattering as he repeated the phrase 'What comes next' each time, the words emerging as a loud shout.

When he finally ceased, and looked back towards the others, blood streamed down his face from multiple gashes and cuts in his flesh. Oddly, he seemed entirely composed. The glitter of madness had not entirely left his eyes, but he appeared to have regained control of himself.

"You gotta remind yourself of the important things around here. You just have to," the Stranger remarked in an even tone, as if nothing unusual had just transpired. He looked past them at the slowly approaching mass out on the plain, indifferent to the blood running steadily down his face. "Time to get going. That is, if you want to survive ... survive so you can survive again, and again, and again, and again...."

He laughed merrily again, as the mania flooded his face once more.

***

"A lesson learned. Now we go!" the Stranger pronounced, as if he were some sort of nonchalant tour guide.

After descending the fire escape, the Stranger had guided them in the direction of the city's outskirts. He had taken the group up to an overpass, to get a closer view of what was coming in from the desert.

"The things I do for my new friends," the Stranger remarked, chuckling. "Always looking out for you, you know!" He laughed aloud once more.

Carlos did not have the will to be irritated with the Stranger. Caught in a stupor, he could not believe what he had just seen. His knuckles were white where they clenched tightly onto the railing of the overpass.

The lines spread across the horizon were just the vanguard of an enormous, incalculable mass of individuals. Thousands upon thousands had flooded into the outer boundaries of the city, enveloping some of the smaller groups of people.

A few of those little bands were still visible from the new position the Stranger had guided Carlos and his companions to. Carlos could see great desperation in the groups of people as they ran about in confusion and fear, trying to evade whatever beings constituted the incalculable horde coming in from the desert plain. His stomach clenched, as he saw the swarming hordes filling in every street and alley, cutting off all routes of escape.

The groups of people in the city were obviously of particular interest to the newcomers. They were methodically encircled, and then converged upon, disappearing from sight in the dense waves of non-distinct figures. Carlos could not make out much detail regarding the tides of new arrivals, but it was readily apparent they were anything but friendly to the denizens of the city.

As the Stranger had implored them to leave, a small group among the scattered bands was being herded into the middle of a street just a few short blocks away.

They were close enough that Carlos could tell that the members of the little band were screaming and crying out desperately for help, standing back to back as they faced the teeming ranks of the incoming flood. Carlos could see a few of the figures trying to fend off the first elements of the horde closing in upon them, until the terrified people were blanketed by the masses rolling in like a dark tide.

"What ... just happened to them ... and who are they?" Darius stammered, staring downward, and clearly shaken by the sight he had witnessed.

"What happened to them isn't something you'd enjoy ... and as far as who they are, well, they aren't really different than you. Just a little more numbed and resigned, I suppose," the Stranger commented evenly, as if he were engaging in nothing more than a casual conversation.

The Stranger started walking away from the overpass, heading to where he could surmount the railing and work his way down the modest slope of ground back to the street level. It was the same way they had climbed up to gain the better vantage.

"As for me, I'm not waiting here. And I don't advise you to either," he called back, swinging his leg over the railing. "We've taken far enough of a risk as it is, lingering as long as we have."

Bracing himself, the Stranger swung his other leg behind him, and disappeared from view.

"Who are they?" asked Darius, hesitating at the railing, and staring at the multitudes slowly working their way towards them.

"I don't know, but it isn't good, Darius. Let's get out of here," Mari commented in a voice thick with anxiety.

Carlos could not turn away as his eyes fell upon someone who staggered through the front of the oncoming throngs, a man screaming at the top of his lungs. He moved laboriously, barely keeping ahead of his relentless pursuers. Carlos saw the struggling figure was covered in blood.

His eyes narrowed as he began to realize there were gouges everywhere on the man, as if he had been bitten and clawed extensively. The next moments confirmed Carlos' initial suspicions, as the man stumbled to the ground.

A couple of his nearest pursuers sank down atop the hapless individual. Without pause, one raised the man's right arm and clamped their teeth into his bare flesh, while the second attacker tore aggressively at the man's right shoulder.

The second figure ripped free a bloody chunk from around the man's neck. Throwing its head back, it stuffed the dripping chunk of meat into its mouth. It was all that Carlos witnessed, as the man was swallowed up moments later by the forefront of the lethal mob.

"Zombies? You gotta be kidding me...." Carlos said, stunned, and wrestling with a tumultuous state of disbelief at seeing a man being eaten alive. "What the hell has happened here?"

"Whatever they are, let's get away from here!" Mari urged, wide-eyed and pulling insistently at Carlos arm.

A few in the grisly crowd then looked up towards the overpass. Carlos's eyes met one of theirs, and he suddenly found himself gazing into an abyss of unending death and misery. Human in form but absent of any shred of humanity, the thing Carlos locked eyes with was a denizen of a terrible realm.

The closer they drew, the more about the incoming horde was revealed to Carlos' eyes. The sickly pallor of their skin was unmistakable. Some had a mottled appearance, as if disease ridden, others were missing large swathes of skin entirely, so as to seem like half-skeletons.

They shuffled, staggered, and dragged themselves along, but there was no mistaking their intent or resolve. They were merciless killers, of a savage, primal kind that no amount of reasoning or bargaining could entreat with.

Carlos felt Darius' hands grab at his wrists, yanking his own hands free from his temporal anchor. "We've gotta get going, man," Darius said. "Let's go now!"

Coming out of his momentary stupor, Carlos followed Darius and Mari as they headed in the direction taken by the Stranger.

The Stranger was nowhere to be seen as they reached the end of the overpass and looked over the railing, evidently having departed the area. Carlos lost his balance on the slope after only a couple of steps, skidding a short distance on his rear before coming to a stop and getting back up. As soon as he reached the bottom and his feet touched the street, he heard a surging cacophony of yells, moans, and screams.

His heart nearly froze in his chest, as the new wave of sound rolled in from behind the overpass. As they had waited and watched, other elements of the gargantuan horde had worked their way inward, reaching the back of the overpass on the lower street level.

"Oh my god!" Mari cried out, eying the peril they were all in.

"Go! Go this way!" Carlos shouted, pointing straight back into the heart of the city. "Go this way now!"

The three broke into a full run down the middle of the street, and Carlos gave no thought to the bizarre rats or flying menaces that had concerned them before. For a time he did not look back, or even look to see how his companions were doing, focusing only on running as fast as he could.

***

Streaming from side streets, a horde brimming with malevolent intent stumbled and trotted into the street. A terrible reek preceded them, saturating the air with the noxious odor of rot and decay.

Carlos, Mari, and Darius kept running as fast as they could, as more and more of the seemingly endless tides began pouring out of the side streets ahead of them. Carlos could not believe anything had managed to get ahead of them, as fast and long as they had been running. Yet it did no good to try and dispute the harsh, stark reality that now faced them.

Darius suddenly cried out, having tripped on something as they pressed to get down the street before the jaws of the vast throng closed shut on their escape route. Carlos rushed back to extend Darius a hand, but the lawyer's face abruptly became a mask of fear as his first step was met with a buckling limp, causing him to crumple to the ground a moment later. He cried out in obvious pain, and Carlos could see that Darius had sprained or broken an ankle.

Carlos looked about, and saw the channel to escape narrowing rapidly ahead. Within moments, they all would become entrapped. The most primal instincts took over; those of self-preservation.

Carlos was a survivor, and one who reacted decisively. Turning his back on Darius, he sprang forward and ran. He did not look back, but he heard Mari's strained breathing and her padding footfalls a moment later, as she raced feverishly after him. Darius began screaming pitifully behind him, a high-pitched sound that chilled Carlos' spirit.

Carlos' heart plummeted and his terror spiked as

more of the zombies came into view, even farther down the street. The light serving as his beacon disappeared, closed off by a solid line of rotting flesh; striding towards him with brutal designs.

To his left, he espied a narrow alleyway that showed no evidence of having any of the horrific creatures within it. Without hesitation, he broke towards the opening, racing across the street and into the mouth of the alleyway. He did not bother to signal to Mari, but she followed close in his wake.

To his great dismay, the alley came to a dead end. Carlos nonetheless ran to the far end, even as he heard the wails and moans of the murderous swarm relentlessly following him and Mari. They swiftly blocked the other end, and started down its length without pause.

"Carlos! What are we going to do? Oh my god … oh my god!" Mari shouted frantically, her face a mask of panic.

"Shut up!" Carlos raged at her, as he looked towards a couple of doors set into the sides of the buildings.

It was either do nothing and be torn apart, or take his chances within one of the buildings. The latter was the more attractive option, by a very wide margin.

Racing back and forth, he found that both of the doors were locked. Glancing down the alley, he viewed the horrid countenances at the forefront of the terrible throng as they shambled to the halfway point of the alleyway.

Some of the figures were without noses, and others without lips, such that their teeth were permanently exposed in a morbid grin. Still others had mangled stubs where an arm should have been. A few pulled themselves across the concrete, unable to stand anymore. There were all manner of horrid disfigurements and wounds exhibited within the freakish rabble, all the results of brutal violence.

The oncoming figures were right out of the heart of Carlos' worst nightmares, and he could feel the insatiable rage driving them. They were creatures governed solely by the primal impulses now guiding them.

With the full force of his heel, Carlos kicked out savagely, knocking off the doorknob of one door, and rupturing the lock. The door limply swung open, as the knob clattered onto the ground. A fragment of relief came to him, as the first of the zombies bearing down upon him reached forward with mangled hands.

Pulling the door fully open, he rushed through, and slammed it shut behind him. He pressed his body against it, putting all of his weight into keeping it closed.

"Carlos! You bastard!" Mari screamed from the other side, her tone one of stunned dismay and abject horror. "Oh god! Oh my god!"

Engrossed in his own concerns, he had not given Mari a moment's thought, but he was not about to risk himself now that he had barely evaded the trap. The moans and howls were deafening from the other side of the door, as her anger immediately turned into full terror. Her screams rose in pitch, becoming an extended screech before cutting off abruptly.

The door then shook forcefully, as it was pounded upon heavily from the other side. Carlos knew he could not hold it forever. He looked about, and saw that there was nothing in range to use to brace or barricade the door with.

The battering on the other side of the door continued without respite, and Carlos felt himself shoved backwards a few inches. He redoubled his efforts to push back, and keep it closed. The attrition was mounting, and he knew that the creatures on the other side would not let up in their efforts.

Taking a deep breath, he threw himself away from the door and ran, hearing the door smash open behind him a few seconds later. Carlos hurried his way through what was a gutted kitchen, inside of an abandoned restaurant. He glanced around quickly, to see if there was a knife or something that could be used as a weapon. The place must have been stripped long before, as there was absolutely nothing of use in sight.

He cursed the fact that he had no time to search, as a burly zombie of over six and a half feet tall emitted a gargling cry and lurched ponderously towards him. Its hair had been ripped out from one side of its head, leaving its skull exposed, and its upper lip gone, giving the creature a fixed expression that was at once grotesque and absurd.

Other partially butchered entities with grayed, swollen flesh streamed in behind the hulking male. Their putrid aroma wafted in with them, causing Carlos to gag.

Carlos burst through the swinging double doors at the forefront of the kitchen, and raced through the wreckage of what had formerly been a broad dining room. Broken tables and chairs littered the space, and Carlos hurried through the assortment of obstacles as best he could.

The broken glass in the facade of the restaurant looked out onto an empty street, and Carlos did not hesitate. He jumped up and hurtled through the front, narrowly missing one large, jagged shard that remained of the windows. Its sharp edge left a mark, scuffing the outside of his left shoe.

Heart pounding, he turned up the street, almost tripping over his feet as he heard the telltale sounds of the approaching masses coming from just ahead. He looked back, and knew that the zombies streaming into the building behind him would be out on the street within mere moments. Down the other way, yet more noises swelled, and he knew the creatures would begin coming into sight within scant seconds.

Seeing one of the ubiquitous piles of refuse and debris strewn all about the city streets, he ran towards it with all the effort he could possibly muster, diving in and pulling all manner of garbage over his body. Burrowing in deeper, he left a very small portal through which he could see into the city street.

His vantage was set at a slightly upward angle, affording him a view down the length of the street and also of the blood-red skies above, the latter framed by the buildings flanking the street.

Just a few short moments later, the street was filled to capacity with the ghastly hordes, and Carlos knew that his only shred of a chance lay in hiding, and keeping completely still. From the noises engulfing his position from all around, he knew he never would have made it out of the street.

Carlos watched helplessly, settling into a mild state of shock as the cadaverous parade shuffled by his makeshift hideaway. Torn, broken, and decayed, the masses of macabre figures were terrifying to behold from up close. Their gaunt eyes, at least those they still possessed as many were missing one or both of those, stared about, devoid of any spark of liveliness or focus. No words came from them, but their mouths emitted wails, moans, and cries that created the chorus of howls that he had heard when the multitudes had approached the city.

One of the figures right before Carlos, remnants of clothes hanging in tatters upon his emaciated build, was lifted up suddenly by a winged entity; of the very kind that had grabbed Jacob earlier. This time, instead of disappearing from sight, the bestial creature hovered about fifteen feet in the air, clutching onto the hapless figure with its back sets of talons driven deep into the graying flesh of its victim's body.

The predatory creature was fully within Carlos' field of view. He was in position to clearly witness the terrible scene that followed, in its repulsive entirety.

Eerie shrieks cut through the air, as two more of the winged creature's kind joined it. They hooked their own rear sets of talons into the flesh of the figure, also driving them in deep such that the three airborne nightmares held the body of the doomed being aloft. Their wings beating steadily, the beasts hovered in place with their immobilized quarry. The being in their grasp moaned loudly, head lolling back and gazing up at one of its tormenters.

With raucous cries, the monstrosities thrust their elongated, skinny arms down, bringing new sets of wickedly-sharp talons to bear as they began tearing into the body vigorously. The figure clearly felt a tremendous degree of pain, crying out in raw agony as the winged creatures levied a merciless, brutal disembowelment upon it. The winged tormentors tossed the contents of the figure's innards over their shoulders, haphazardly discarding everything they ripped out. Set against the backdrop of the crimson skies, the sight was a lucid nightmare for Carlos to behold.

As he beheld the ferocious spectacle, Carlos discerned it was the act of dismemberment that drove the creatures, and not any desire for sustenance. The realization froze Carlos to the core, as he watched one of the entities tear the figure's right arm loose from its socket, tossing the severed limb down into the masses of living death that filled the streets below. Carlos did not even want to consider what had happened to Jacob.

Once the victim had been entirely dismembered, the three winged creatures uttered shrill, raucous cries, and flapped away. Carlos stared at the spot where they had been for a few moments, before bringing his gaze back down to the abominations on the street level.

What shook Carlos the most was that the masses of rotting beings were not just going after those like himself, who still seemed to possess a full awareness and physical vitality. Individuals walking alongside another would just as suddenly beset their neighbor as they would continue to shuffle and stagger onward. Acts of savage violence, and even macabre lust, permeated the decaying horde.

There was no rhyme or reason to the behavior of those comprising the revenant hordes. It was simply an incessant display of violence in all of its grisly forms, and the creatures involved showed no regard for the others of their kind.

Disgust and revulsion rose up in Carlos, filling him with a dizzying nausea that caused him to wretch. He had to close his eyes as two female zombies, who had once been quite voluptuous, judging from their still-present curves, bore an older male figure down to the ground.

The older man could do nothing to stop them, as he

had no arms left to fend them off. They clawed at him repeatedly, tearing away his flesh. When he moaned and cried, one of his assailants bit out his throat.

The two female figures screeched, as if working themselves into a frenzy. One of them suddenly ripped at his groin, her blood-soaked hand coming free with a hideous trophy clutched within it. Even more sickening, she proceeded to consume it.

A stab of delirium and shock struck Carlos as the male figure's face seemed to stare right into his hiding place. He recognized the figure immediately, an elderly banking magnate who had financed more than a few of Carlos' business projects. The man had hosted many a gala at his opulent mansion, located upon a sprawling estate adorned with the finest of luxuries.

He had always been steeped in various perversions, spending a fortune on young women, and other, far more disturbing carnal pursuits. Carlos knew the billionaire had never envisioned being torn to pieces and consumed alive by a pair of formerly attractive females, beings now far steeped in decay, and awash with murderous, pitiless intent.

More than once, Carlos felt sharp stabs of panic and fear as other zombies tumbled into the large pile of debris, or were born down into it as the result of an assault by another of their rapacious kind. Several times the putrefying figures came dangerously close to exposing his concealed position, their acrid stench almost causing him to audibly gag. It was all that he could do to keep still and quiet, but he knew he would be ripped apart, torn limb from limb the moment his hiding place was uncovered.

Wholly nauseated, Carlos stared transfixed as a male and female zombie began to copulate on the hood of an abandoned car sitting only a few feet from where he lay. The damage already done to the bodies of both participants rendered them largely unable to consummate. Their rutting, decrepit forms, rubbing decayed flesh and pus-filled wounds together, was a vile mockery of an act serving as the genesis of new life.

For the first time in his entire life, Carlos saw through lust to the purity present in the sexual act, a sanctity entirely absent within the revolting simulacrum now being performed before his eyes. He had never seen or understood it in such a way before, until he had so starkly witnessed its total absence.

The thrusting, grunting male suddenly found his head and upper torso engulfed within slavering jaws that tore half of his body free. Shreds of flesh and blood were tossed all about the area, spraying gore everywhere, such that even Carlos felt a few drops of gristle splatter onto his face. He stifled a cry of terror as he beheld a giant, macabre, wolf-like head swallow the head and torso of the male in just a few pronounced gulps.

Fear stilled Carlos' breath within his chest as one long, jointed leg, covered with short hairs, stepped into sight, followed by another, and then several more. The creature with the wolfish-head was huge and utterly bizarre, with a massive, swollen body resembling that of a great spider.

Its legs were each twice again as tall as an average man, and its body was covered in a layer of coarse bristles. It walked over the vehicle, its swollen belly raking across the prone female zombie, who was still covered from the waist down by the inert remains of the half-eaten male.

Carlos' heart raced impossibly fast, as one of the spidery legs came within just an arm's length of him. He did not want to face the blood-soaked maw of the horrifying creature, his nostrils filling with the fetid scent accompanying the surreal beast.

Finished with its grisly morsel, and to Carlos' tremendous relief, the beast strode onward, the ends of its eight legs clattering upon the hot pavement. The monster then halted and raised one forward appendage. Skewering another of the zombies from behind, the wolf and spider hybrid pinned its victim in place, as its long muzzle lowered to resume its gruesome feast.

Behind the creature, the female that had been under the male at the time of the attack finally began to move. She awkwardly shrugged off the hips and legs of the male that had been half-consumed. Her eyes were listless where Carlos could see them through her strands of stringy, matted hair, hanging in tatters mingled with scarred patches of bare skin. Her body was streaked with fresh, oozing wounds from the bristles that had been dragged across her by the giant, spidery beast.

No sooner had she managed to wobble back to her feet than a slithering nightmare coiled about her with blazing speed. Her eyes looked upwards dully, largely unresponsive as they stared into the gaping maw of the serpentine beast now holding her rigidly in place.

The creature had an elongated, humanoid face, with enormous fangs, and solid, blood-red eyes. She did not even utter a single protest or bleat of fear as the beast's jaws distended, covered her, and began to swallow her whole.

The wolf-and-spider hybrid, and the serpent-creature, were only the beginning of a large number of strange and terrifying creatures that Carlos witnessed, as the masses of zombies began stumbling and trudging onward.

Carlos could perceive the shift in their purpose, as the attacks that the zombie-things levied upon each other dwindled swiftly. Some primal element deep within them had begun to surface at last, compelling them to motion for the purpose of self-preservation.

As the concerted movement began, it was as if they were being hounded by a wave of predators, imbued with insatiable appetites. Carlos trembled where he lay, cool sweat pouring in rivulets down his face, a hapless spectator fearful of discovery at any given moment. There was nowhere to run to, as the pile of refuse he had taken cover in was ensconced within the midst of a horrific swarm of flesh eaters.

All manner of distortions and combinations were displayed among the grisly onslaught, with not one of the new monstrosities directly resembling any living creature Carlos had ever seen before. After what seemed like an interminably long period of time, Carlos finally sensed an urgency manifesting in the various creatures gorging themselves on the nearly endless multitudes of zombies. There seemed to be no sating the appetites of the newcomers, just as there had been no relief for the things in the first wave.

A distinct change began to gradually emerge, as the second wave of predators started moving onward themselves. The area around Carlos was steadily emptied, save for a few lingering zombies whose broken, mutilated forms were physically incapable of moving onward.

Carlos finally risked a few adjustments to gain a better vantage, after enduring what he perceived to be a very long time in which he had not seen or heard any sign of the larger predators or the zombie hordes. The streets outside the refuse pile were disturbingly quiet, broken only by a few periodic howls or wails.

Crawling slowly out of the pile of debris he had burrowed into, he brushed himself off as he looked up and down the streets. Thankfully, they were almost entirely empty, though covered in all manner of fleshy remains and severed body parts.

Carlos felt his leg grabbed weakly, looking down to see the upper half of a woman who was trying to gnaw upon his ankle. Carlos vented his fear and anger into a bludgeoning kick that knocked out the few remaining teeth she possessed.

She had few distinctive features, as she had been ripped up and chewed on all over. Enraged, Carlos stamped down upon her head again and again, crushing her skull beneath his heel and splattering her brains out onto the pavement.

It was then that he took notice of a diamond pendant that had been freed in the burst of violence. It was one he had bestowed as a gift to his main receptionist many years before; a receptionist he had abandoned to a horrific fate in an alleyway clogged by ravenous entities.

Carlos yanked his eyes away, hurriedly scraping the gore on his shoes off. He did not even want to think about what had just happened, as he trudged forward and headed down the street. He ignored the sluggish moans from a couple of zombies that were far too incapacitated to be of any threat to him.

He moved through streets similarly filled with the gruesome aftermath of the horde, and the swarm of outlandish beasts that had followed in their wake. His shoes squished and sloshed as he crossed some stretches of ground, and he rigidly averted his eyes from peering at the sources of the noises.

At last, he reached the edge of the cursed city,

and stared off towards the horizon. He felt the ground reverberating beneath his feet, and his heart quailed.

In the far distance, shadowy hulks loomed, already growing larger as he watched. The vision heralded the approach of beings of gargantuan sizes, of a scale Carlos could barely believe to be possible. He did not want to speculate on the forms they would have, having just witnessed the ghastly parade flowing through the city.

A strange thought came to him, like an interior inspiration, as he continued watching the colossi approach. In the world he had lived for forty-six years, Carlos was much like the titans he espied approaching from the distance.

Everything had been beneath him, a bounty for him to partake of at his choosing. He had been at the apex, a man who even very powerful individuals hesitated to cross. He had wielded power over the mass rabble and the prominent alike, all tools for him to exploit.

The only difference was that this was a much purer world. The stronger consumed the weaker, to be consumed in turn by those even greater. Perhaps there were things even mightier than the oncoming titans he now witnessed.

It was all a reflection of the natural essence of the world that he had left behind, now being displayed in its most pristine sense, raw and uninhibited by any sense of compassion, mercy, or generosity. Such dispositions as the latter had no place where one could pursue the hungers gaping inside without inhibition or restraint.

"Hahahahahahaha!"

The boisterous laughter sliced through Carlos' rumination, and he looked over to see the Stranger grinning broadly at him. The eyes of the Stranger exuded madness, but the blood and cuts that had been all over his face were now gone; the skin returned back to an unsullied state.

"Lost some companions, did you? Don't worry, they'll be back. Might take an age, but you can't escape into oblivion here!" the Stranger commented brightly. "Enduring existence - you'll savor every moment of it."

Carlos did not reply, staring sullenly at the Stranger. His thoughts were a swirl of fear, confusion, and despair.

"Speechless? I'm not surprised. You saw quite a lot, didn't you? Incredible, wasn't it?" the Stranger asked him merrily, as if they had just shared a grand experience together. He then pointed towards the horizon. "And those lads out there, just wait until you get a better look at them. Oh ... you wait and see! Incredible sights they are. Simply incredible! Just don't get caught up by them!"

Again, Carlos said nothing.

"Not much for words, are you? Well, you want to know something?" the Stranger asked him.

Carlos did not so much as nod, or utter a word.

"This place is just a tiny, tiny, infinitesimal part of the realms you now have available to explore. You have all the time in the world to see the sights ... that is, if you can keep in one piece," the Stranger said with a chuckle.

Striding a few feet over, he kicked a decapitated head high into the air, the mouth and eyes still moving as it thudded into the brick wall of a nearby building.

"Don't end up like that one, or it might be eons before you have an awareness like you do now, if you are lucky," the Stranger stated casually. He looked towards Carlos and smiled. "Well, I gotta get going. I know you will miss me for now, but cheer up, sooner or later we'll probably run into each other again, no matter how vast these realms are.

"We've got forever, you know! And you earned this permanent vacation! You chose this destination. Don't forget that, my friend! Can't buy, cajole, argue, or spin your way out of this one! You've got yourself infinite real estate to explore and experience! Enjoy it, to the fullest extent!"

The Stranger grinned, chortling as he started off with a brisk, lively step, heading into the depths of the city. After he had gone a short distance, he stopped abruptly, and called back over his shoulder, "Just remember ... here it's all about what comes next!"

The piercing laughter of the Stranger echoed in the streets and alleys behind, as Carlos remained fixed in place. He turned his eyes towards the shadowy forms approaching the city.

A sickening feeling settled into Carlos as he watched the distant giants drawing closer. He could see multilegged forms, bipedal ones, and slithering ones, all on an unbelievably massive scale.

In that instance, he realized his place in this gruesome new world, a place where he could not age; a state of existence in which there was no time.

Now he was the lowliest of prey, no different than the hapless creatures he once flung into his predator fish tank for amusement. As the ground shook beneath his feet and the behemoths loomed even closer, Carlos could not avoid thinking of the small creatures he had cast into a tank where only violent death awaited them.

There was no way out of the place he now found himself in. Though he might move around and evade doom for a time, he could not avoid the predators in this realm forever.

He had already witnessed his eventual fate, the moment he had stomped down upon Mari's head. He realized bitterly that such a fate was inevitable.

At some point, he would likely be counted among those numbed, decaying multitudes, herded and hounded along by monstrosities that were themselves mere fodder for what came behind them. He was no longer a physical being, but rather a spiritual being with physical attributes; all enhanced for the purpose of pain and suffering. He would be eaten, bludgeoned, and torn apart, decaying to nothing, just to find himself doing it all over again.

"What comes next... what comes next... what comes

next," Carlos said in rapid succession, dropping to his knees, and slamming his head into the pavement. He laughed aloud, a mania gripping him as he felt blood streaking down his face. "Where in the hell am I?... Got the first part of that question right ... hell is where I am!"

A deafening bellow filled the skies, accompanying a tremor running through the ground. Carlos laughed again, this time with full force, the sound devoid of humor and acutely echoing the tone of the Stranger. Carlos was truly the smallest of fish now, fated to swim forever within a sea of ravenous predators.

DROWNING IN TEARS

DROWNING IN TEARS

"Despair often breeds disease."
- Sophocles

Resembling a stark lattice-work, the intertwining branches of leafless trees encompassing the path lent a naked, desolate feel to the surroundings. Shadows pooled and shifted everywhere, frequently appearing to move on their own accord. There was just enough ambient light to see for a fair distance, though the source of the enduring twilight was impossible to determine.

Jared paused for a few moments, turning his eyes upward, peering towards the raging sky. Streaked with dark crimson tendrils, the sky rolled incessantly, carrying the promise of a violent storm about to break.

Without foliage, the trees around him offered no hope of cover for the deluge poised to fall at any given moment. No thunder sounded as of yet, and no lightning broke the underbelly of the cloud masses, so perhaps there was still a little time.

How he had come to the shadowy forest, he could not remember. His mind was shrouded within a misty haze. It was hard to do anything more than observe and react, though snippets of clarity flashed from time to time in his head, as he continued down the debris-strewn, dirt pathway.

Darting a glance to the right, he looked just in time to see a black, amorphous shape, resembling clustered swirls of smoke, drifting along the ground. It curled around a tree in its path, and hovered for a few moments. Jared felt everything within him tense at the sight of the enigmatic shape, though the feeling ebbed as the murky form flowed onward, heading deeper into the bizarre, sprawling woodlands.

It was not the first time he had felt such anxiety, seeing shadows behaving in ways he did not think possible. In truth, a clinging fear had accompanied him all along the woodland path, as well as a chasm of sadness deep within.

He could barely remember the bright flash and sound of thunder, both promising him refuge from the abyss of sorrow enveloping him from the moment Kayla was taken from him. She was his world, and when she left his foundations had been torn asunder. The days and weeks afterward had been a malaise of anger and mourning, with everything cast in a gray, lifeless pall.

Life itself had become maddening and insufferable, driving him steadily towards a moment of liberation. That shining instant had been conducted with only thoughts of Kayla embraced in his mind and heart.

Now he found himself wandering though a grotesque forest with its host of dynamic shadows, unaware of how he got there, or even where he was going. Something skittered to his right, scuffling along the forest floor, though it did not sound large enough to be of any concern. He gave the movements little thought, as terribly hollow as he felt inside, though the shadows continued to unnerve him.

"Wanderer of Sorrow, where are you going?" a breathy, sibilant voice with a feminine quality called out to him.

The words enfolded him, sounding as if they came from everywhere at once. Jared stopped, turning in place to see the speaker of the words, though nothing met his eyes but stooped, crooked trees immersed in deep shadows.

"See what you were meant to see," the soothing tone came again, beckoning with an undercurrent of promise.

Turning about again, he saw the outline of a figure in the path a short distance ahead of him. From the shapely curves revealed by a long, white gown, and the tumbling cascade of curls flowing about the figure's shoulders, Jared knew he looked upon a woman; though her face was veiled in dark shadow.

She was tall, at least a head higher than he was,

and radiated a confident aura. Quietly, she awaited his response.

"What I was meant to see?" Jared asked hesitantly, his brow furrowing as he tried to fathom the words of the strange woman. "What do you mean?"

She started moving towards him, though the grace of her step, and her steady pace, made it seem as if she drifted just above the surface. He looked upon her in wonder and curiosity.

"Some were meant for pain, others for sorrow, and others for consummation, and even rebirth. Though none that wander these realms will ever see the Light that falls upon another place," she told him, drawing nearer.

Though much closer, she remained enigmatic in nature. He could make little out about her features. It was as if anything about her face he tried to focus upon thwarted his vision, muddling his comprehension.

Only the soft white light glowing about her eyes registered with him. His efforts to scrutinize her were entirely stymied when she came to a halt and turned her back upon him.

"You brave great dangers in this place, and you do so unnecessarily," she said. "Come with me, and find what you seek."

Jared readied to follow, and then paused for a moment. "Who are you?"

"You may call me The Patron," she answered, a hint of bemusement in her tone as she began moving forward.

Jared looked around briefly, espying yet another of the shadowy, shapeless forms off to the left. Feeling a spike in anxiety as his eyes beheld the black, misty form, he decided to follow closely in her wake.

"Where are we, right now?" he asked, picking up his pace to try and draw closer to her. He fell farther behind, but could do nothing to move faster. "It seems I'm not myself at the moment."

"You are more yourself than you ever have been, Jared. As for where we are, we are nowhere ... and everywhere. Both are true enough," she replied enigmatically. She moved with the kind of relaxed ease that showed no concerns whatsoever about what dwelled in the woods.

Her words perplexed him, but he was not about to abandon pressing for some answers. "I have no idea how I even got here, wherever this place is," Jared said. "I definitely don't recognize it."

"You know. You simply choose not to accept," she said, a strange lilt to her voice.

"No, I don't know," Jared retorted, sounding more defiant than he had intended. "And I'm not really in any mood to care, anyways."

"Loss ... in realms of loss immeasurable ... perhaps that is what may grant you self-determination in this ... place ... as you call it," she said.

He looked towards the bottom of her white gown, which appeared to lightly brush the pathway. He could not see her feet, and it still appeared as if she was drifting down the path.

She kept pulling farther ahead, and like some dream he could not will his limbs to move any faster. It was as if she moved through air and he through water. Anxiety began to blossom inside and spread throughout him.

Without giving him any advance indication, she turned suddenly to the right, heading off the pathway entirely. Jared kept moving down the path, wondering what she was up to. He could see her easily enough, a ghostly white form surrounded by murk.

Feeling an icy, prickly sensation along the back of his neck, Jared turned his head and looked up towards a low ridge. Outlined against the sky, standing a short distance before one of the skeletal trees, was an enormous, lupine shape. Shaggy fur hung low from its great muzzle, and its eyes glowed, embers in the gloom, as the creature stared unblinking towards him.

When he looked back, his guide was nowhere in sight. Jared spurred himself forward with all his will, to where he finally saw where the strange woman had turned off the main pathway. A small trail snaked off into the trees, heading down a long slope.

A low, rumbling growl sounded from the direction of the creature on the ridge, and Jared set foot on the pathway and hurried along it as best he could. After several steps, he began to panic, as there still was no trace of the woman. The anxiety drove him to hustle faster, and he almost tripped over his feet as he emerged from the trees and broke into open ground.

In a natural basin formed by the encompassing slopes, a broad, shimmering pool was spread before Jared's eyes. At once, he felt drawn towards it, and thoughts of the woman he had been trying to find faded.

Slowly, he edged closer to the water, reaching the lip of the pool and staring into its caliginous depths. Everything about him seemed to become heavier with each passing moment, as he continued gazing into the blackness.

Whether minutes or hours later, as he could not grasp any sense of time, something began to happen within the pool. The waters began to gradually clear, a silvery light appearing from within its far depths.

Jared gave a start as he saw a figure rising towards him out of the blackness. To his surprise, he recognized that it was a woman, and at first he wondered if it was the mysterious guide from the forest.

Tresses of hair billowed slowly from the spectral woman's head, and her arms were outstretched, as if reaching out towards him. He stood transfixed, spellbound by what he was witnessing.

A whirlwind of emotions rushed through him as her face broke the surface of the water, flooding him with recognition. Her lustrous green eyes peered towards him, unblinking and casting an enveloping gaze.

Astounded at the miraculous revelation, he watched

as she rose above the water, setting her bare feet down lightly upon the surface of the glimmering pool. She started towards him, walking upon the water. Her skin shined as drops of the water coursed down her supple body, to rejoin the dark liquid beneath.

"Kayla?" Jared finally managed to whisper, shaking uncontrollably with thunderous emotions.

"You have found me, my love," she told him in a soft voice, drawing near the water's edge. "Beyond time itself, you have found me."

As she drew closer, he noticed something strange about the quality of her eyes, but Jared was so overcome with feelings that he could do little more than wait for her to come to him. In his mind, he could remember the open casket, and the cold, hard grave he had visited hundreds of time, draped in the shadows of an old maple tree. Yet here she was, vibrant, alive, and in the fullness of health, walking across water.

His knees gave out, and he slumped down, an acolyte kneeling before his goddess. Jared watched her every step as tears streamed from his eyes, experiencing a moment he never imagined to be possible.

She neared the bank. "We cannot remain what we were, Jared," she said to him in a gentle voice, as she stepped onto the ground. "We must become, and accept."

"Oh Kayla, I ... I thought ... " he stammered, as tears continued to run down his face. It took an act of will to even say the words. "I thought you died ... "

"Shhhhh ... there is no need to cry, Jared," Kayla responded. "We are together again."

Reaching down, she took his hands and helped him to his feet, as he struggled to contain his emotions. Sliding her arms around him, she drew him into a deep, lingering kiss. The taste of her was exquisite, even electrifying, a precious sensation Jared had thought he would never experience again.

He had left the world behind of his own accord, determined to become a voyager into realms unknown. Oblivion or something else awaited, but never in a million years could he have guessed he would have been reunited with Kayla so soon.

When their lips parted at last, Kayla's green eyes held his gaze, piercing him with the intensity reflected within. She repeated the words she had spoken as she crossed the water, this time a little more firmly. "We cannot remain what we were. We must become, and accept."

"What ... what do you mean?" Jared asked her, lightheaded, and still feeling weak in his knees.

Everything he desired was right before his eyes, alive once again, and returned to him. He could not imagine needing anything else, and her words confused him.

"Take your clothes off," Kayla said gently, the hint of a smile dancing about her full, soft lips.

Jared nodded, even as he felt the stirrings of arousal

at her words. They had immersed in the throes of lust as often as they had embraced in love, but no matter how they gave their bodies to each other, it was never enough for him to just be inside her.

Another desire had always beckoned to him, always seeming just out of reach. He had always wanted to meld with her completely, in spirit and body, and truly become one flesh.

Slowly, he began to remove his clothes, first his shirt, then his shoes, socks, jeans, and finally his underwear. He discarded them in a loose pile by the side of the pool.

Jared felt no discomfort standing naked before Kayla, and not a thought came into his mind about being so exposed in the midst of a macabre forest, brimming with living shadows and menacing beasts. His mind was entirely consumed with the woman before him.

"Before you take a path of becoming, you must first be baptized," Kayla said, with a somber edge.

"Baptized?" Jared responded, with a little surprise. Religion had never claimed a place in either of their worlds, and it was very strange to hear such a word coming from her lips.

"You must trust me ... baptized in a new way, unlike the world we left," Kayla said, a little more gently.

Jared just nodded, knowing he would have done anything she asked. A warm breeze rippled across the pool, caressing his skin with its soft touch.

"Get into the pool," she told him. "And give yourself

over to what comes."

At her instruction, he stepped into the water, or at least that was what he thought it was until he had gone a few feet out from the bank and became more immersed in the salty liquid. As he stepped off the edge of the pool and began to tread the water, Jared noticed there was a strange, viscous quality to the dark substance. He did not know what to make of it at first, but understanding came into his mind like the breaking of dawn on the horizon.

The waters were the essence of sorrow and lament, a lake of tears in the purest sense; tears resonating with those he had shed endlessly in the weeks and months following Kayla's death. All of it fell upon him at once, savagely rending his spirit apart, and inflicting a piercing anguish.

Breath fled him, and his head lowered beneath the surface as the dense liquid drew him downward and flooded into his body. He could not resist as he sank lower into the dark depths, a leaden heaviness pervading him.

Every moment of despair, touch of helplessness, and icy shard of loneliness converged, opening chasms of suffering within him. Shadowy images paraded through his mind, flickers of memories of days spent with Kayla, leading to the cataclysmic day her body had been overcome by the mass of substances she had willingly put into it.

He lived through everything again, magnified a

hundred-fold in its intensity. Jared could not shed enough tears to reflect the depths of grief he experienced within the dark embrace of the pool.

The last image emerging clearly within his mind was the moment he had placed a barrel of cold steel into his mouth, seeking oblivion or a way to search after Kayla in another realm. He realized he had achieved both his death and the reunion he sought, though the nature of the two things had turned out very differently than anything he had imagined. He sank lower and lower, with no sense of direction in the lightless depths.

The sorrow was beyond overwhelming, and finally he let go of all traces of hope, resigning himself entirely to the darkness. For a flicker of a moment, a frigid coldness seized him, and oblivion filled his spirit.

The horrid sensation passed quickly enough, and conscious awareness returned. As it did, he felt himself began to rise slowly, drifting upwards through the blackness.

Faint light reached his eyes at last, as the ponderous weight ebbed slowly from his body. The surface drew nearer, as if it was pulling him up, until his head finally broke free from the dense liquid.

With some exertion, he maneuvered towards the shore, finding his footing in the shallower area near the embankment. With a laborious heave, he pulled himself from the pool.

Flopping heavily upon the shore, Jared was barely

able to roll onto his back. His body felt utterly exhausted, entirely sapped by the intensive experience.

Looking upward, he saw that Kayla was standing over him, her head framed by the violet, churning cloud masses far above. She extended him the hint of a grin, but her eyes still carried that odd quality which had jarred him a little before he entered the waters of the pool.

Kayla stepped over him, and lowered herself down, her knees pressing into the soft ground by his hips. Gazing up at her naked form, and feeling her body on top of him, it took little effort to inflame his arousal.

Reaching down, she wasted little time in guiding him into her. With a low moan, which to Jared's ears sounded layered, as if made by more than one voice, she leaned her head back.

Building towards a pulsing rhythm, she soon drew him into ecstasy. Peering downward, she leaned in closer, as her heat gripped him lower. Jared closed his eyes, succumbing to the intense pleasures rippling throughout his body, like nothing he had ever felt before.

Her tongue flicked out to touch his ear, and he felt her breath upon his skin. As the rough texture brushed his lobe, he opened his eyes again. He flinched, as her eyes were impenetrable obsidian, faceted and glinting, her gaze burrowing into his own.

She kept her hips moving in a slow gyration as he stared back at her in surprise. "An emptiness will always remain within you, in this place," she whispered, in a husky voice. "You must shed what you once were, to be reborn. You must become, if you wish to journey across the worlds with me. This you must willingly accept. Do you cast your own will aside, to become?"

Weakly, he nodded, but his intent to accept her invitation was clear within his mind. Despite her unsettling change in appearance, he was willing to do anything she asked of him. His response seemed to please her greatly, as a grin spread wide on her lips, and a strange, sparkling look came into her eyes.

Her lips then parted, and her jaws spread apart, unnaturally wide. Great fangs were exposed within her mouth, but they retracted, as if sliding into sheaths. Jared took notice of another row of teeth, lined evenly, the upper surface containing a razor-sharp edge.

Though shocked at the development, it was as if he was hypnotized. He could do nothing but watch helplessly, and he realized what it meant to abdicate the power of his own will.

Placing her mouth upon his chest, as if to kiss him, he felt agonizing stabs of pain as she sheared off a large slice of his skin. He shuddered with a melding of pain and pleasure, as she resumed with more pronounced force where he was still deep inside of her. The heat built to the edge of a burning sensation around his groin, far exceeding any sensation he had felt there before.

She closed her eyes, a look of great pleasure spread upon her face as she chewed upon the piece of his skin, and then proceeded to swallow it. He felt his mind going dizzy, and he tensed as she lowered her head again.

A trace of fear entered his mind and began to spread, but he did nothing to resist her. A part of him fathomed that he could not resist her, even if he had wanted to. Beyond the matter of his subjugated will, he felt her strength, and knew it was far greater than his own.

"It is what must be, if you are to go forth with me into realms unexplored," she told him. She brought her right hand before his eyes, and he saw talons, her hands now elongated claws.

With no change of expression, she drew the talons along the side of his face, in a gentle caress. The passage of the talons sheared the skin right off his left cheek.

"All is communion, as I eat of your flesh, and drink of your blood," she stated with a smile, bringing the shred of skin to her mouth, and eating it.

Again and again, she sliced off more of his skin, as bleeding patches became wide swathes of exposed veins and muscle. Using her mouth and fingers, she worked over his chest, and then his shoulders, neck and face.

She continued to draw sensual pleasure from her actions, her movements intensifying as she continued with the gruesome repast. Jared was paralyzed in a perfect balance of pain and pleasure, a compliant witness to the destruction of his own body.

Eventually, Kayla pulled off of him, as she worked her way lower down his body. Delirious agony soared alongside the consuming passion, rising towards the heights of a macabre ecstasy.

By the time she rolled him over, the pain he felt was excruciating, with every last nerve in his body laid bare. He trembled as she continued using her talons and teeth to strip the skin from every last part of his body.

At long last, she rolled him onto his back once more, having reduced him to a bleeding, shuddering, and skinless lump of tendons, bones, and meat. Unable to blink, Jared could do nothing to shut his sight off, as she had not spared even the lids of his eyes.

His vision clouded with a bloody film, Jared could only vaguely make out her right hand, as she raised it upward. Her fingers now looked impossibly long, and the talons at the end had extended considerably.

Without warning, she drove her hand downward, ripping into his chest. With a vigorous wrenching of her arm, she tore out his heart, and gorged upon it ravenously. In that moment, she looked more bestial than human, a savage, demonic thing governed by hunger and lust. During that same moment, he realized he was no better.

All the blood draining out from him drenched the ground beneath, leaking not only his life essence but the fluids of the drowning pool. A searing acid leeching from his spirit's deepest, innermost reservoirs, the substance of all the sorrows and pain he had long carried within him soaked into the soil.

After what seemed like an age, he was thoroughly

empty.   Lying upon the ground, little more than an emptied husk, Jared still remained conscious.

His energy was gone, and he knew what had just happened had not been done to a physical body, or he would have long since been spared the agonies by unconsciousness and death.   Rather, his soul had taken form, and been thoroughly ravished and drained.

Jared could not muster enough willpower to see what had become of Kayla.   He had no desire, or any other feeling, beyond the encompassing hollowness.

More harrowing, he knew he could not die.   His body was bereft of blood, but that no longer mattered in the state of existence he now found himself in.

He could do nothing when he heard the scuffling steps of unnameable creatures approaching.   Hisses and raspy breaths accompanied prodding muzzles and claws, as the things rooted around his body.

Again made to bear witness to his own demise, Jared experienced every tear and bite as the brutish things ripped chunks of flesh from him.   He could hear their large teeth scraping against his bones as they took what they wanted.   Jared was nothing more than carrion, left for scavengers to feast upon.

Lost in growing darkness, ages could have passed and it would have made no difference to Jared.   Time no longer mattered, he knew, but he wondered if this was the fate he was forever resigned to.

On two occasions his clouded gaze beheld skeletal

wraiths hovering over him, but they never stayed for very long. He got the impression they savored what was happening to him, judging by their leering expressions, formed from desiccated skin stretched across misshapen skulls.

The flap of leathery wings heralded another kind of tormentor. Strange, winged denizens of the murky forest joined in the grisly feast, finally taking Jared's sight away as the sharp-beaked things plucked out his eyes.

At first, the thought of having no vision panicked him terribly, but eventually he found he did not have the will to worry any more. He did not even care when a final cluster of porcine beasts from the dark forest arrived and began crushing his bones in their heavy jaws.

Starting with Kayla's stripping of his skin, his bodily form was the forest's communion, consumed to the last. His thoughts slowed to a trickle, until he was empty of mind once again, and cast into oblivion.

***

Roused from abyssal depths of consciousness, a powerful energy began flowing throughout his being. It jarred him unmercifully from his extended limbo, restoring a sense of form that had been cast aside during his internment within nothingness.

It was not unlike the moment when he had been drawn upward through the viscous liquid of the dark pool. Something was summoning him back, pulling him towards another surface.

He arched his back and screamed piteously, feeling the equivalent of a thousand shards of glass digging slowly into his back. The voice that emerged from him was different than the one he had possessed before. Grating and deeper, it had the layered quality that he had noticed in Kayla. Light seeped back through eyes newly formed, taking in the vision of a violet, rolling cloud mass.

"Rise anew, my love," Kayla's voice came to him, as if calling out from a tremendous distance.

Jared blinked, and realized more things about him had changed. He glanced down at the silvery sheen of his new skin, which looked to be moonlight transformed into flesh. He stared upon it in wonder, having no idea how the transformation had come to pass.

"What was, is no more … and what is, will always be," Kayla said, extending her taloned hand towards him, as she stepped fully into his sight.

Her face largely retained the appearance she had in her human life, but other aspects of her form had changed profoundly. She was taller, and winged, and her skin had a scaly quality. Her eyes remained obsidian pools, pitiless orbs devoid of reflecting other emotions.

Beyond the pain he felt in his new form, he could feel nothing as she drew him up to his feet. A nascent pair of wings sprouted from his back, and then expanded, causing him to clench his teeth in the extreme pain of transformation.

He understood that he could never have a feeling of joy or love again. Those things were alien to the new realm he found himself within.

Other emotions were possible, such as lust or rage, but for the moment all he felt was a pervading numbness. He had drowned in his tears, and shed everything he had been. A new creation, he was now suited well for realms of nightmare and lament.

He knew where he was, and he accepted it fully. Jared had chosen his home forever. That absolute finality gave him a strange sense of resolve.

Yet fear was not absent, as he was only beginning to understand the enormity of his choice. Like rage and sorrow, fear was another of the emotions that held primacy in the shadow-cloaked realms where he now dwelled.

He knew without a doubt he would come to know fear very intimately. Not wanting to think upon that at the present moment, he shoved the troubling realization to the back of his mind.

"Come, my love, let's fly," Kayla invited with a whisper not unlike a hiss. She spread her lips in a semblance of a smile, exposing the lengthy fangs that had returned to their former positions.

"Yes, let's fly," Jared agreed, feeling his gums splitting as sharp fangs broke through.

Together, Jared and Kayla spread their wings and

took to the skies, swiftly leaving the pool far behind. Flying came natural and he had no difficulty keeping pace with her.

From the top of a ridge-line not far from the pool, a hulking, wolfish creature and a ghostly woman gazed upon the couple. Both were well-pleased with the creations the two souls had become within their forest.

At great heights where only wraiths flew to and fro, Jared and Kayla were soon traversing the black night over the sprawling forest, a landscape teeming with all manner of horrors. Jagged mountains of staggering height loomed ahead, calling the flying pair onward.

Jared looked down upon the trees as he heard faint cries and screams from the shadows below. To his momentary surprise, he found the wails of terror and desperation remarkably delightful.

It was a revealing moment, when he knew what Kayla had meant regarding becoming. He was already a new being, and he was evolving into something more.

He glanced over to Kayla and saw a look of great pleasure on her face as she took in the cries and shrieks. Then, as he listened, he attuned further to his surroundings.

The cries melded into a kind of music, no longer a cacophony but more an exquisite orchestration. Though he felt cold inside, so very cold, he smiled broadly; knowing this was just the first realm they would explore together on an endless journey of the darkest kind.

LORDS OF WAR

LORDS OF WAR

"Never think that war, no matter how necessary, nor how justified, is not a crime."
-Ernest Hemingway

A panorama of desolation seeped into Dalton's eyes. Scorching, sulfuric breezes wafted across the barren wasteland stretching to the far horizon.

The undulating terrain spanned a broad range of elevations. Some rises were as high as great hills, interspersed with stretches of low ground riddled with all manner of smoldering crevices, holes, and gullies. Wisps of acrid, black smoke drifted across the landscape, pooling into thick masses in some areas, while thinning in others.

Standing atop one of the hill-like rises, Dalton Rockefeller peered into the distance. A state of indecision pervaded him. He had no inkling of where he was, or where he should go.

Dalton grimaced and gagged as another wave of

stench enveloped him, the rancid odor conspicuously like burning flesh. The periodic, encompassing blasts of pungency were driven by the hot winds coursing through the barrenness, but he could not determine the source of the nauseating odors.

Off to the right were a smattering of brighter elements, set within a dark swathe of flatter terrain, the latter ringed by several low ridges and hills. Dalton wondered what the reddish, flaring lights represented. They were too far in the distance for him to make out any details.

Floating and swirling in the breezes, gray flakes settled upon him, continuing the steady, downward cascade from the billowing cloud masses far above. It was as if the entire sky was cloaked in layers of churning ash, a gray and black canopy devoid of any hint of what lay beyond. A low, sustained growl of thunder occasionally rippled through the rolling ash-clouds, as if a simmering anger hovered over the inhospitable region.

Without a watch, and with no sun or moon to mark the passage of time, Dalton had no idea how long he remained in place upon the summit, staring silently into the ashen terrain. Finally, he willed his limbs to move. Setting off down the slope, he headed in the direction of the flickering lights.

Glancing around at scattered tufts of blackened brush, he pondered the charred remains of foliage, wondering what manner of terrible cataclysm had so thoroughly devastated the land. Reaching the bottom of the hill, he set forth at a quickened pace, eager to get through the desolate area as soon as he could.

Searching his mind, he wondered what place this was, and how he had gotten there, but turned up nothing. The lack of answers vexed him as he continued forward.

Something tugged at the edges of his mind, but the thoughts were like dark phantoms. Evasive and ephemeral, they eluded his grasp, even as they tormented him with the promise of answers.

It was like some barrier had been firmly set in place, preventing him from accessing his own memories. Something deep inside kept telling him they were all still there, it was just that he could not unlock those inner vaults. Recognition of the quandary only angered him further.

"Secretary Rockefeller!" a voice hailed abruptly, cutting through the thick air and halting him in his tracks.

Turning his head, Dalton saw two figures striding towards him. One he did not know, while the other's countenance was well familiar.

"Secretary Carville?" Dalton questioned the latter of the two, the lilt in his voice betraying his shock at seeing the woman.

He was a little surprised that he had clearly recognized her, as he could not remember much of anything from so much as a day, or even a few hours, ago. The impenetrable wall erected between his consciousness and memories allowed only a few small bits and pieces to trickle through, but what little he gleaned was far from enough to make any sense of the world around him.

Helen Carville looked more disheveled and tattered than he had ever seen her before. Her usually immaculate business suit was torn in many places, riddled with stains and dirt ground deeply into the expensive fabric.

Normally, not a single strand of hair on her head lay out of place. Now, the disheveled woman looked as if someone had tousled her hair, before wiping soot and grime across her face.

It was hard to believe this was the same woman who had addressed security councils at the United Nations, negotiated international treaties, and guided coalitions in global missions. One of the highest authorities in the United States government, she had been one of the most powerful women in the world.

"Dalton, I can't say I'm surprised to see you here," she responded wearily, her voice sounding hollow. Her face remained sullen, and she did not muster even the slightest grin at seeing him.

He found he was surprised at the reaction, and flashing memories of her laughing and smiling broadly at him paraded through his mind. The clarity of the memories gave him pause, for it was as if something else had summoned them for a purpose.

Looking closer, Dalton saw the signs of deep exhaustion written everywhere upon her. Her figure, usually carried high and proud, was slouched in posture, and darkened, baggy skin surrounded her eyes. She was an echo of the powerful, confident woman he had known for decades.

"Secretary Rockefeller, it is so good to see you here. I have been looking all over for you," the third individual stated, interjecting into their conversation. "In this place, that is no easy thing, believe me. I could search for the equivalent of thousands of years, and still find no sign of you. But I have found you, and the sight of you here gladdens me more than you can ever understand."

Though the stranger smiled, and his words were casual, there was not even a splinter of light-heartedness about him. His eyes were steel-cold, and his tone devoid of any shred of warmth.

He was a young man, perhaps about thirty years old, with the squared jaw, low-cropped hair, and general air indicative of a military man or member of law enforcement. Dalton had been surrounded by the type all his life, quite ubiquitously during the years he had served the president as his Secretary of Defense.

"Then maybe you can tell me where we are," Dalton replied, dryly. "If you know so much about this godforsaken place."

A sparkle of mirth glittered for a moment in the eyes of the younger man. "Well stated, Dalton Rockefeller, and I think you'll figure everything out soon enough. New arrivals are always a little foggy. But realization comes in time, and it is always an exciting moment for me to watch it happen. I admit, it will be a lot for you to take in, and might be a little overwhelming, even for a man who possessed such high authority and dealt with so many large scale events."

"A real smart-ass, I see," Dalton retorted curtly, glowering at the man. Indignant at being addressed so brazenly by a man who obviously ranked far beneath him, he felt ire welling swiftly from within.

"He's the only one who can guide you though this place, Dalton," Helen interrupted sharply. "Believe me, you do not want to wander this place by yourself."

Dalton did not miss the nervous, fearful edge to her voice, nor the anxious look she cast towards the young man. It did not dull his irritation, but it warned him towards caution.

"Is that so?" Dalton asked evenly of the man.

"It all depends," the man replied. He shrugged his shoulders nonchalantly, and looked around. "In a way, we've got all the time, and all the space, you could ever want. There are no limits here, Secretary Rockefeller. We have forever, in a very real sense."

"Then why would I need a guide, if I have all the time and space I want?" Dalton riposted, flippant. "Don't waste my time. Get to the point and speak to me in direct terms."

"I am, Dalton. That's what you fail to understand now," the man replied, with an icy smile. "You speak of wasting your time, but I can't waste what isn't there to waste. Listen carefully, I said we have all the time and space you could ever want ... in a way."

The self-assured look on the man's face unsettled him, but Dalton's right hand balled up into a fist. He greatly desired to smash his fist into the other man's face, and knock the smugness right out of him. No subordinate had ever dared to speak to him like this man.

"You want to hit me? Go right ahead, if it makes you feel better," the stranger invited. He spread his arms out wide, and grinned. "Hit me to your heart's content, Dalton."

"Not worth the effort," Dalton snapped. He stormed past the man, resuming his forward trek, leaving the other two behind.

"By all means, don't let me delay you. I see you were heading towards those beacons in the distance," the man called out from behind. "I would be very, very careful about those if I were you. Just a little friendly advice."

"I don't need any advice from you," Dalton roared, without looking back. He added, after a couple moments. "Helen, I don't know what's gotten into you, but you are more than welcome to come along. Or, you can stay with that insipid fool."

He kept his face fixed toward the beacons, even when it was clear there would be no reply from her. Keeping a robust stride maintained, he continued towards the lights, the hard soles of his shoes crunching against the parched ground.

Cognizance danced maddeningly at the edges of his mind again, wraiths flitting just beyond his inner grasp. Seeing Helen Carville invoked some memories, but nothing that gave an inkling of an idea as to where he was, or how he had gotten there. He could only hope the beacons led to some kind of answer.

***

Dalton slowed to a halt, staring in disbelief and revulsion towards the first beacon, now that it was close enough for him to examine in detail. The light he had seen from afar emitted from a raging fire, blazing vigorously around the blackened flesh of a man whose wrists and ankles were bound in iron manacles. Lengths of black chain secured the unfortunate figure to the rocky ground.

Though the man's body was scorched all over, and every last hair had been singed off, he was fully conscious. His eyes bulged out, mouth agape, spread in a silent scream as he writhed and twisted about in the savage, tormenting flames.

"Some beacon there, if that's what you thought it was," muttered a familiar voice. "Who would want to be drawn to this? I'll take that back, there are more than a few in this existence that would. They are not the kind you really want to meet, Dalton."

Dalton flinched at the abrupt intrusion, and whirled

about to face the young man he had left behind, who had followed unbidden with Helen at his side. His blood immediately surged to a boil with the hot anger he felt looking at the man.

"Did I ask you anything? What are you doing here?" Dalton pressed, glaring at the young man. "Why have you followed me? Get away from me!"

He took a step towards him, eyes narrowing. His hands curled into fists, tendrils of rage working their way through him.

The young man gazed towards Dalton, showing no concern at Dalton's posture as the mocking smile returned to his face. He asked calmly, "Recognize anyone here?"

"Recognize who? Helen?" Dalton shot back. "I think I'm damn well familiar with her. And I sure as hell don't know you."

"Look a little closer into the flames, Dalton," the young man invited him, the corners of his lips turning up farther.

At the prompt, Dalton turned his attention back towards the burning man. He looked closer at the anguished figure trapped within the flames. It was then that he locked eyes with the hapless individual.

"General Collins" Dalton stammered, his blood running from fire to ice, as several pieces of memory stepped forth from the mists of his mind to form a coherent image.

One of the highest-ranking figures in the military,

General Collins had been in charge of air operations within a range of nations, from the Middle East, to Asia, Africa, and even South America. Drones and manned aircraft alike had executed countless operations under his command.

Pronouncing death and destruction upon numerous villages and towns, he was a man who had decided the fate of so many. For every insurgent who had fallen, so had a man, woman, or child who were swept into the category of collateral damage.

Recognition flared in the weeping eyes of the general, his face contorted in terrible agony. Dalton could not begin to imagine the torment the man suffered.

The heat from the fire beat strongly against Dalton's face. After taking a couple of steps forward, he found it unbearable to draw even one step closer to the hapless general.

"What kind of madness is this?" Dalton growled at the young man, backing up a few paces from the fire. "This is a man of the utmost distinction, who served his country dutifully."

"Yes, he served his country. Very dutifully in fact," the young man replied, plainly unruffled by Dalton's caustic demeanor. "Highly lauded. Lots of medals. Very distinguished, at least in the eyes of the world. A man of great influence. Respected by many. I cannot argue any of that with you, Dalton. But those are not the measures used to decide one's destination. The dead that you deemed collateral damage are not just statistics when it comes to using other measures."

"He needs to be freed from there!" Dalton shouted indignantly, unnerved further by the young man's impassive disposition. It was an outrage that a man such as General Collins was being subjected to such a horrific torment, though it never entered Dalton's mind to ask how the general was surviving the blazing fires. Any normal man wreathed in such a fire would have been dead within moments.

"Be my guest," the young man responded, with a casual shrug. "I won't stop you from freeing him. Go right in, and take the chains off him. I must caution you that the links are very strong. The general's adherence to duty in his life gave those links their strength, as his sense of duty overpowered any considerations of morality. Isn't that right Helen? You understand, don't you?"

The young man looked to the woman, and Dalton did not miss the trembling in her body. Her fearful reaction to the other man's words bothered him, but the general was in immediate need of his help.

Dalton tried again to edge closer to the flames, but the blistering heat rose sharply with just two steps. He simply could not approach within twenty paces of the beleaguered general due to the withering flames, as the heat they generated was far too intense to endure.

Looking about, Dalton saw nothing that could be used to aid the man, or even put him beyond his misery.

If he had a gun, he would have used it in an act of mercy upon the general, but a rocky wasteland encompassed them, offering nothing.

Dalton stood in place and gazed upon the tortured man, swarmed by the horror and surreal nature of what he witnessed before him. The burning general's survival should have been impossible. He should have been reduced to ash, but beyond charring his flesh the flames did nothing further to his bodily form.

Dalton turned away from the wretched general. His gaze drifted towards the other beacons, and the pit in his stomach sunk into a deeper abyss. He realized the beacons all consisted of similarly chained, burning figures.

His steps were shuffling and heavy as he moved away from the general, unable to concentrate his severely rattled thoughts. Dalton ambled listlessly in the direction of another beacon, though his gaze was not fixed upon the trapped figure there.

Scuffling footsteps preceded Helen's voice. While her tone sounded tired and thin, urgency laced her words. "He told you not to come here Dalton. You should have listened to him. It is not safe here. It is not really safe anywhere, but you need to listen to him. You can spare yourself some terrors."

"Who ... who chained them?" Dalton mumbled.

"We are not alone in this place," Helen replied. "There are dangers everywhere."

Despite the oppressive heat, Dalton felt a frigid chill

pass through him. He caught the tone of implication in her words, and knew she indicated something far beyond his comprehension.

"Who is that man with you?" Dalton asked her.

"I know him only as the Soldier," Helen answered.

"You seem like you know him very well," Dalton said.

Helen nodded, but said nothing.

"What … is this place?" Dalton asked, right before he stumbled with the sudden shaking of the ground.

"Oh no!" Helen exclaimed, with a strong tenor of fright.

"Lay low, over here," the Soldier called sharply from the right.

The intensity in the tremors rapidly increased, and some small fragment of self-preservation snapped Dalton out of his dazed stupor. He blinked his eyes, and began to look around to see if he could espy the cause of the tumult.

"Get over here, now!" the Soldier commanded.

Dalton felt himself yanked aside, as Helen grabbed onto him with desperate strength. "You fool!" she exclaimed. "It may be too late!"

He let himself be pulled along with her, picking up his pace as the two hurried towards the Soldier. The ground vibrated more intensely, upsetting his balance. The Soldier guided them towards a jagged rock protruding out of the ground, set close to another of the burning, chained figures.

The ground shook more forcefully underneath, and Dalton and Helen just barely made it behind the rock when a fearsome sight met his eyes. Blanching, he saw a gigantic creature tromping right by the rock he was crouched by. The bulky monstrosity towered over him, at least fifty feet in height.

It was headed straight towards the inferno. Covered in rows of triangular scutes and dark scales, the brawny, long-limbed creature was a nightmarish entity to behold. It walked on two legs, and had an extended set of jaws dripping with saliva.

Grabbing the flame-shrouded man with both arms, and yanking powerfully upward, the creature ripped the man free of his shackles. Without hands or feet, the man was lifted higher from the ground, his limbs ending in nothing more than ragged, bloody stumps. His seared head was brought eye to eye with the demonic giant holding him.

The scaly horror showed no discomfort at the flames, which died down as it clutched the maimed figure. Dalton got the sickening sense it was dragging out the inevitable, in a very intentional way.

The creature's baleful gaze bore into the man, even as its huge maw opened, loosing an ear-splitting roar. The man's face was a mask of delirious terror, and his mouth opened in what would have been a piercing scream had he been able to make any sound.

The creature lifted the man towards its gaping maw,

bringing him in slowly, head first. When his upper torso was fully within the jaws of the creature, it snapped them down with tremendous force. The upper half of the man's body was sheared off. The creature patiently held onto the lower portion, blood dripping while it chewed and swallowed its first bite.

Stuffing the legs down into its gullet, the creature finished off the remains of the man. Its grisly meal concluded, the creature trudged onward, the ground jarring with each massive step.

It headed straight for General Collins, and Dalton turned his eyes away. He did not want to witness the awful fate of the general. Keeping his eyes averted, he heard the creatures roar again, followed soon after with more of its ground-reverberating steps.

Dalton felt an icy tinge at the nape of his neck. He glanced up in time to see a vast, winged shape gliding upon the air currents far above them. Its form blended well with the black and gray skies, and he had a difficult time discerning its exact shape. Whatever it was, he hoped it took no notice of his group.

"Time to continue onward," the Soldier said evenly. "Or do you wish to ignore my advice again? You can, and you will find out quickly how far it gets you."

Dalton did not argue, desiring to get as far as away from the dismaying place as he could. He hurried after Helen and the Soldier as they started away from the sheltering rock.

The ground no longer rumbled, but he cast several looks upward, feeling highly-exposed as they crossed the arid terrain. He felt like he was some sort of small beast scurrying out from cover, underneath skies containing the most deadly kind of hawks.

***

Though they encountered no more of the surreal beacons, the plains seemed to stretch on indefinitely. Dalton kept his legs moving, doing what he could to keep up with Helen and the Soldier, who strode with purposeful steps at their lead.

The monotony was finally broken when they entered an area littered with parched, withered brush. Dalton had the sense of things scuttling about just off the periphery of his vision, which spurred him to keep up with the Soldier.

At long last they passed through the brush-dotted region and entered another swathe of parched soil. The Soldier brought they to a halt a few steps into the new area.

"Wait," he said, staring ahead.

In a few moments, a curious sight came into view. A lone, naked man was running hard across the rocky plain while being pursued by a horde of snakes. The slithering mass kept right at his heels. If there was one stumble or trip, the man would be overcome by his pursuers.

The man drew nearer, bringing his features into closer view. Dalton froze in place. As with General Collins, he recognized the man being harrowed by the serpents. Wesley Barton was the chief executive officer of a company that manufactured attack drones.

Dalton had spent more than one evening relaxing on the man's yacht as it traversed the eastern coast, or the warmer waters of the Carribean. There was no trace of his disarming smile or cocky edge now. He had the look of a beaten, terrified man.

As Dalton looked onward, Wesley stumbled and fell to his knees, and the pursuing swarm of serpents engulfed him. Burrowing into his flesh, they wormed throughout his body, emerging in sprays of flesh and blood. Two burst through his eyes, and one through his mouth, as he collapsed upon the ground.

A swarm of buzzing flies draped over him as the serpents abruptly scattered. In a matter of moments, the dark mass reduced his remains to nothingness.

"It is an ill-fate, but one he forged," the Soldier observed in a calm tone. "Flies and serpents are given life here for each and every death resulting from his life's work. They continue to multiply as his debt continues to grow. The seeds he planted in his life bring ever greater harvests, and he can do nothing to stop it here."

A small cyclone of dust churned in the place where the man had been destroyed. More and more dust whipped within the circular winds, becoming a dense mass that finally dissipated to reveal Wesley once again, reformed in the flesh.

Wesley looked towards Dalton, and recognition came to his eyes. "Dalton! Dalton, oh god, please help me ... please help me. I need heeeeelllp!"

A loud hissing filled the air, from all directions. Everywhere Dalton looked serpents were emerging from the ground. Without hesitation, the black, sinuous shapes began winding their way towards Wesley, tongues flicking out and eyes locked on their quarry. Not one of them paid any heed to the Soldier, Helen, or Dalton.

Terror filled the man's face, and he kept crying out to Dalton and his companions, but finally had to run as the serpents drew closer. The chase began once again as the snakes picked up speed, in a pursuit that would end in the same grisly fashion Dalton had just witnessed.

A sharp thought cut through the fear and shock pervading Dalton. The drones Wesley Barton's company manufactured had resulted in the deaths of thousands, which lead to many more, as disease, poverty, and other evils thriving in the wake of war exacted a continuing toll. What had brought him luxury and comfort in his other life now bestowed a growing legion of terrors. Dalton did not even want to contemplate the hordes of living torments descending upon the hapless man.

"Who are you really? What are you?" Dalton screamed at the Soldier, as a glimmer of realization threatened to undermine his sanity. He got the distinct notion that he was in another world entirely, though what it was exactly he could not say.

A cold smile came to the Soldier's face. "You can call me the Soldier. But I am just a Witness. And I have been waiting for you."

"You? Waiting for me?" Dalton asked. "For what purpose?"

"You will see, soon enough," the Soldier replied. "Let's go, it is not much farther now."

"Not much farther to what? Where are we going?" Dalton queried.

"You are a man of war, Dalton," the Soldier stated. "Don't you want to see the Lords of War?"

"I just want to get away from here," Dalton said, and for the first time an edge of desperation crept into his voice.

The Soldier nodded. "We have nothing to fear from the things that afflict that man. Let us continue forward."

The Soldier stepped forward, followed by Helen and Dalton. As he walked across the ground, he thought of the burning general, the snake-riddle Wesley Barton, and then the gaunt, haunted-looking Helen Carville.

He had been in league with them in all kinds of matters throughout his years at the heights of government. Dalton had regularly aided and abetted their actions and initiatives; supporting, defending, and condoning the three at every turn.

The thoughts evoked a feeling of dread that shrouded

him like a clammy chill. If the general's life had merited the torments of a searing fire and the jaws of a slavering monstrosity, and Wesley's had earned him a host of flesh-burrowing serpents, then whatever might be lying in wait for Dalton could well be even worse. It was difficult to even conceive of something exceeding the suffering of the two men.

He barely staved off a wave of panic as they continued forward, and took a little heart from the fact that Helen was not being tortured or harried. The emptiness in her eyes and haggard appearance spoke volumes that not all had been well with her experience, but she was certainly not in the dire predicaments of the two men he had witnessed.

An urge to speak with her further pressed from within, but he did not want the Soldier to overhear any of his thoughts. The more he was around the enigmatic figure, the more his unease grew. There was something about the man that tied to both Helen and himself, but like the problems with his memory, he could not get a firm grasp upon it.

A gust of extremely hot winds coursed over him, making him wince and clench his teeth in the suffocating heat. In a few moments it was gone, and the crunching steps of the three replaced the whistling air in his ears.

His two companions showed no outward reaction. The Soldier's lack of response was one matter, but the fact that Helen treated the scorching winds with indifference unnerved him further.

He knew that answers would eventually be forthcoming, but he was not so sure he wanted that time to arrive. In truth, he began to feel that the less he knew, and the less he remembered, the better off he was.

***

"Go ahead, have yourself a good look," the Soldier invited, beckoning him forward. The mocking edge was sharp in his guide's voice. "Feast your eyes on all of this."

Dalton crept hesitantly to the rocky edge and peered downward. His breath caught instantly in his throat at the extraordinary scene revealed to his eyes.

Far below, within the massive basin, numerous ebon figures of tremendous size were gathered. Wraith-like, the substance of their dark forms were misty and flowing, with only faintly defined shapes.

The air surrounding the basin was freezing to the touch, and Dalton had the distinct impression that the cold did not come from the atmosphere. Rather, it derived from the throng of enormous spectral entities. He could only imagine what it felt like nearer to them, as his vantage was situated at a great distance.

A phenomenon in the skies drew Dalton's attention upward. He shuddered in the embrace of the cold, but his focus was riveted on the event he was witnessing.

Far above, the rolling cloud masses were parted,

creating a clear opening. A great vortex swirled in the gap, and within its center was a broiling inferno.

As Dalton looked upon the expanding scene in a state of awe, a blinding light flashed within the vortex, like a thousand lightning bolts. Several of the black shapes in the rocky basin shot into the skies, swiftly absorbed by the vortex. A deep, thunderous roar accompanied their ascent, the power of the ravenous cries causing Dalton to shake uncontrollably.

The chilling sounds were the voices of the entities themselves, speaking words in some foreign tongue. Jubilation reverberated through the tones he heard, accompanied by a frenzied hunger.

"What ... what are ... those ... things?" Dalton finally managed to stammer, a few moments after several of the huge wraiths had vanished into the center of the churning vortex.

"Spirits with a mission, Dalton. Very powerful, ancient spirits. Oh, that's right, you didn't think such were real, so this is all new to you. Well, for now just know they cannot go into the world through any power of their own ... Secretary Rockefeller," the Soldier commented at his side. His smile and voice carried a scornful quality, particularly as he gave Dalton's title and surname. "No, they require the assistance of free will, and free action, which invites them into the world you were born in. Once there they can poison it with undying wickedness, and cultivate a harvest of sorrows."

Dalton shook his head. "Ridiculous. You expect me to believe that those ... things ... are called forth by people? Nothing like that ever existed and you know it. I may be having some difficulties at the moment, but I know in my heart I never saw anything like that before. You just seek to fool me, but I am no imbecile, Soldier. Find one who is more gullible towards your illusions."

This time, it was Dalton's words that dripped with mockery and contempt. He glared at the Soldier, feeling a raw hatred towards the man.

"Eyes see so very little," the Soldier replied nonchalantly. "Let me help you see what you loosed into the world. For it was your own free will, Dalton, that enabled creatures such as these to leave this realm behind. You opened the gates into your world for many of these spirits."

As if a mental dam crumbled, a mass of images flooded into Dalton's mind. Few of the visions were called from the vaults of his memory. It was an invasion of his thoughts that no effort of his could dispel. He was compelled to witness each and every sequence that emerged, in the fullness of clarity.

Shiny corridors, air-conditioned offices, and immaculately kept grounds warded by high-tech security demarcated the places where life was bestowed upon wars all over the globe. Stations all throughout the military complexes were effectively thrones of judgment, where the fates of so many were decided with cold precision.

Secured networks carried orders across the world, relayed from the gleaming sentinels in orbit far above the surface of the earth. Calm night skies draped across foreign lands would soon have missiles streaking through them, as well as a host of metallic birds of prey, brimming with lethality.

In the waters lurked massive leviathans, which at a word could disgorge missiles that could reduce a robust building to rubble in mere seconds. Prowling the seas, such vessels had carried out many directives given by Dalton Rockefeller.

Overlapping the images and viewed clearly, as if the only things before his gaze, another sequence played out. Very different in nature than the undersea display and other military elements preceding it, the new vision depicted the same place he beheld from the edge of the basin.

As the commands rolled out in that other world, and the first booms and rumbles shook the earth, a thousand upon a thousand lightning streaks shot out from the center of the vortex and rippled through the sky. Swarms of the great wraiths – thousands in number - bellowed and howled as they rushed into the air.

The air shook with the force of their upward passage. Dalton quailed as he saw the masses of darkness blot out the center of the vortex, before disappearing into the fiery midst an instant later.

"Does Iraq ring a bell with you?" the Soldier said. "Oh the things you and others set in motion with that one. The earth received hosts of demonic spirits from here, all because of what you unleashed there. You gave them passage. Do you understand a little better now?"

Dalton said nothing, taken aback at the smile now on the Soldier's face. It had a decidedly feral quality, like some beast bearing its fangs.

He blinked his eyes and forced himself to control his straying thoughts. The last thing he was going to do was allow the other man to play more with his mind.

"I have seen quite enough," Dalton said, backing away from the edge. He stood up and looked towards Helen, who had kept back the entire time. She did not meet his eyes as he spoke to her. "Helen, this is all ridiculous. You can stay here if you choose, but I want to get away from here."

She said nothing in reply, looking downward. Helen had the look of a beaten individual, a far cry from the supremely confident, often haughty woman he had known for decades.

"What is wrong with you!" he snapped.

"Tell me, Dalton, where will you go?" she said after a few more moments of pensive silence.

Her words, low and calm, still stabbed into him. He knew he had no answer for her, and the feelings of panic began to muster at the edges of his consciousness.

"Don't you know anything about this place?" he

asked her.

"More than I care to know," Helen replied sullenly, bringing her eyes up. They sparked with a crazed edge, as her voice rose in volume. "And I know I still haven't even scratched the surface of this place! I know I am going to find out a lot more, and so are you!"

"She speaks the truth, Dalton," the Soldier interjected calmly. "But be my guest, go take a walk, and maybe you can get a few more answers."

Helen laughed, but it was a sound devoid of merriment. To Dalton's eyes, it was as if she were having some sort of breakdown and going mad right before his eyes.

"Answers! Yes, Dalton, find the answers you seek!" she shrieked at him, as tears began to run from her eyes. "Go, go now and find them! Go, Dalton!"

The emotional outburst took him off guard, and a part of him feared that the commotion would rouse the attention of the things down in the basin. "Shut up, Helen! Do you want those things to know we are here?"

She laughed all the louder. "They do not care, Dalton. They want to go into the world, through gates opened by people like you and me! You and I are here now, right where they want us, and millions and millions more!"

"Where is here then, Helen? Where is here?" Dalton pressed.

She seemed as if she were about to reply, but the

Soldier cut her off. "No, Helen, he must come to his own conclusion!"

As if he were an authority over her, Helen became silent immediately.

"You are taking orders from this clown? What has gotten into you, Helen?" Dalton asked, casting a sharp glance at the soldier for interrupting.

"Just go, Dalton ... You'll get a few more answers, I assure you," the Soldier told him. "Here, let me be of some assistance, to get you going on your path of self-discovery."

***

Faster than Dalton could blink, he found himself alone, in the midst of a far different terrain than the one he had been trekking through with Helen and the Soldier. A bizarre wetland radiated in every direction.

A haphazard grid of raised ground formed the borders of pools of stagnant, mucky water. The pools of water were in all manner of shapes and sizes. A low mist hung a short distance above Dalton's head.

Worse, he was alone. There was no sign of Helen or the Soldier.

"What now?" Dalton muttered irritably, thinking of the Soldier.

A low wailing sounded from far off to his right, and then an undulating moan from behind. Something akin to a howl wafted through the thick air from his left.

Several more eerie, guttural cries emerged, filling the air. Yet wherever Dalton looked he could see nothing but pools and the low ceiling of mist.

As the chilling chorus surrounded him, the sounds of sloshing water rose from close by. Dalton turned his head in the direction of the noise, his eyes widening at the horror rising from the pool.

His gaze locked in place upon the pool, even as several other liquid bodies around him began to stir. Breaking the surface and orienting in Dalton's direction were a number of macabre entities. The grimy water in the pools looked to be shallow, ranging from the knees to the waist on the ghastly beings.

Dalton's eyes then swept the area around him. A horrid feeling of alarm rose swiftly as he took in the sight of figures rising up in every direction. There was no clear channel through them; he was effectively surrounded.

Emerging from the viscous muck, numerous entities crawled up from steep embankments, out onto the land. With glops of glistening sludge sliding off their shambling forms, the beings slowly began trudging towards Dalton.

The beings did not look human, except in the most vague sense of having arms, legs, a head and a body. Their overly large heads looked far too bulky for their thin, fragile-looking necks. Bulbous eyes were fixated squarely upon Dalton, the orbs containing malevolent gazes filled with a simmering rage.

Desiccated, leathery skin covered their elongated, bony limbs, and only their distended bellies prevented them from looking entirely like flesh-draped skeletons.

The things made no sound, but when they opened their mouths they exposed lines of teeth that looked as if they had been filed into short spikes. Their jaws were far too large for any human, bestowing their faces with a freakish sense of distortion. The revenants were of all sizes, ranging from small children, to adolescents, to adults, some of whom were a full head taller in stature than Dalton.

"And what could this be?" came a familiar voice.

Dalton turned quickly towards the Soldier, who was standing atop an embankment several pools away. The man showed no concern for the creatures nearing him. For their part, they seemed not to notice the Soldier at all.

"What is this? Get me out of here! You put me here, didn't you? Get me out!" Dalton shouted, the words coming out fast in his panic. "What are you waiting for? Stop this!"

"Ha Ha Ha Ha!" laughed the Soldier, seeming to be highly amused at the manifesting peril and Dalton's hysteria.

"What the hell are you laughing about?" Dalton shrieked anxiously. "Get me out of here!"

Dalton began shuffling in one direction and then another, indecisively. His mind fixated on escape, every path he saw ran straight into one or more of the repulsive beings. There appeared to be no escape, heightening his panic as the dripping revenants sloshed and stumbled towards him.

"Cripple nations, destroy the lives of thousands upon thousands, and you are foolish enough to think it gives birth to nothing?" The Soldier said to Dalton, staring at him with a look of incredulity. "Do you really think nothing came of your sanctions? Nothing came of your … agreements, and negotiations? You have long sown the seeds for quite a harvest, Secretary Rockefeller. Just as those complicit with you are now reaping theirs …."

Dalton immediately thought back to the two Generals, Helen, and the others he had come across while traversing the hellish landscape. Full understanding came to him in a flash.

"Let's get out of here!" Dalton said with desperation, turning around and gazing upon the hopeless situation.

His heart leaped, as he identified a single path that looked clear. Without a moment's hesitation, be broke into a run along the pathway. Lurching revenants grabbed at him from the pools to either side, but he was just high enough above the pools to evade their grasp.

"Why leave? This is all of your own making. It is your turn to reap!" the Soldier shouted after him, breaking into a bout of maniacal laughter.

Dalton kept moving as the laughter faded behind him. Many figures had shuffled and shambled several paces out from the pools ahead of him, but the open channel through their midst still beckoned.

He ran as hard as he could, his panic rising as macabre figures closed in upon either side. A terrible stench filled his nostrils as the decaying horde pressed ever closer, the ravenous hunger in their gazes spurring him forward with desperation.

Dalton slowed as he saw a pair of the entities close off the channel a little farther ahead. Their forms had been concealed until they had crested the embankments of pools to either side of the raised pathway.

He cursed his luck, delirious with anxiety. A sound to his right drew his attention, and he whipped his head about to see another of the things staggering up a low incline.

A large form flashed by him, as a heavy blow was delivered to the emaciated being reaching out for him. "I'm not turning you loose, not just yet!" the Soldier exclaimed. Whirling about and throwing a thunderous right cross, the Soldier sent another entity tumbling back across the pathway and down into the pool. Dalton gasped, seeing that the thing had come up behind him and gotten to within arm's length.

The Soldier grabbed forcefully onto Dalton, nearly pulling him from his feet as he started forward. Dalton had no explanation for the intervention, as the man who was so recently gripped by madness became his savior in mere moments.

The Soldier plowed through the revenants ahead of them. Dalton marveled at the raw demonstration of the Soldier's blinding speed and skill. He was suddenly glad he had not tried to strike the Soldier earlier.

Somehow they made it through the last of the figures, fleeing in haste. Dalton saw no choice other than to follow in the wake of The Soldier, as he had no idea as to where to go or where they were.

He blinked in surprise, looking upon a parched, barren scene. Dalton was no longer surrounded by mist and the maze of muck and pools. Adding to the mystery, the Soldier was nowhere to be seen.

A promise of threat coursed through the air as a hot wind howled in his ears. Turning about in place, Dalton saw he was in some manner of village nestled amongst towering mountains.

No sign of movement or life could be found anywhere. Dalton's shoes scraped against the dry ground as he stepped forward, wondering where he was.

A hazy pall was draped across the sky, and he could see no indication of a sun. Though a gloom reigned over mountains and valley alike, there was still plenty of ambiance to see by.

Dalton's nerves were on edge as he continued forward. The location resembled any number of places in Afghanistan he had seen during his life; both in person and on surveillance monitors bringing intelligence or documenting military strikes.

Walking into the center of the rubble and burned-out husks of dwellings, Dalton's heart jumped as he heard a low wailing begin to mount. The sound rose and swirled all about him, thickening as if the initial tone was being joined by other tendrils. Dalton came to a stop, and turned around, unable to ascertain the cause of the eerie noises. Raspy, guttural, and hollow, the hellish chorus evoked a permeating dread within him.

Breaking free of loose soil mounded a few paces to the right, a hand clutched at the air. The sight froze Dalton rigidly in place, and his mind spun fast.

There was no flesh upon the skeletal appendage. It was followed by a bony arm, and then another, as something unnatural began to scrape and pull itself from the debris.

Dalton stood transfixed, as a garish figure emerged from the pile. Tattered strips of clothing hung from some ribs, but not an ounce of flesh clung to its bones from the neck down.

From the neck up, the face of a nine or ten year-old child gazed at him, expressionless and sullen. Its flesh was gray and puffy, a decaying substance accenting its sunken eyes and thin, drawn lips. The eyes of the figure were light gray in hue, rheumy and glassy all over their surfaces.

Dalton was transfixed at the sight of the thing. Whatever animated the morbid entity was not governed by the laws of nature he had known.

"Youuuuu are stained with the deathhhhh of allllllll," the thing pronounced in a hissing, breathy voice. "As the one who died only lived a portionnnn of hissss own life, mossssst of my body is gone in thissss place. It is youuuuu who are the causssse of it."

Dalton took a couple of steps back, staring in incredulity at the horrifying child-being whose form defied all manner of logic. He could make no sense of its words either, as he struggled to process the things he saw.

"How can a child be in this place? How can you be alive?" Dalton asked plaintively. He continued to step backwards, maintaining the distance between himself and the freakish being.

"The child?" the being asked in a changing tone of voice, its words sounding like wind rushing through a cave. "I am no spirit of the living ... I am a spirit born of death. You gave birth to me."

Dalton turned about to run, only to trip over his own feet as he saw a solid line of entities arrayed behind him. All of them, man, woman and child alike, shared the same manner of appearance as the one addressing him.

Still others were emerging from the ground, forming out of swirls of dust, or coming out from behind the destroyed village buildings.

"Youuuuuu gave birth to usssss!" the child-thing called with an unmistakable air of accusation.

Another flash of understanding shot through

his mind. The things teeming around him were representations of those who had died in violence under his express authority. The collateral damage statistics had manifested into monsters; diabolic entities of Dalton's own making.

Off to his left, Dalton eyed what looked to be a cliff's edge. Only four of the beings were standing in that area, though two more were breaking out from the ground, and yet another forming from swirls of dust.

Before he was hemmed in on all sides and trapped, he ran towards the cliff. Shifting to the right, he kept free of the entities as they moved to intercept him. The edge of the cliff approached fast, as desperation consumed all his thoughts.

Dalton did not see the jagged boundary of the cliff that rushed up to meet his frantic step. He kicked out into empty space, his arms flailing wildly as his legs failed to find support underneath him. Tumbling headlong down the face of the cliff, Dalton screamed as he plummeted hundreds upon hundreds of feet.

A parched, rocky surface awaited his fall, and his cries were cut off abruptly as he struck the unforgiving ground. Every limb in his body was pierced with a blinding, intensive pain, as if every bone had been crushed to bits.

After an unknown time had passed, Dalton opened his eyes. He slowly lifted his head up from the ground, astounded that he was still conscious. His vision was still sharp, though sight was anything but a gift as he beheld the terrifying sight encompassing him.

Sprawling masses of figures were tearing each other apart, gouging, clawing, and biting as they furiously assaulted one another. Terrible wounds had been inflicted upon many. Some were missing limbs, others had been savagely disemboweled, and still others exhibited horrific burns.

Dalton's mind spun as he watched a headless body raining heavy-fisted blows upon its opponent lying prone on the ground. A sickening crack sounded as one particularly thunderous blow landed upon the sternum of the other figure. Dalton blanched as the next blow drove deep down into the other's chest, breaking completely through its rib cage.

Dalton remained transfixed, unable to move anything other than his head. Panic spiraled as he saw a few of the combatants cease fighting, and begin to turn their heads in his direction. Stumbling and limping, several began making their way towards him.

From the pieces of clothing still clinging to many bodies, and the visages that remained largely intact, Dalton realized a great number of the figures were once human. They derived from all nations, and all armies from across time.

Another bolt of clarity struck him, as he came to understand that these were the warriors with the darkest of hearts. Consumed with violence, they no longer fought for any single land or populace. Former enemies were now united in a delirium of war fever, indulging their insatiable rages upon that infernal battlefield; murderous spirits enshrined in a semblance of flesh and blood.

Massive, bulky forms moved amongst the grotesque multitudes, as did great serpentine shapes, leaving swathes of destruction in their paths. Overhead, shrieking and roaring, were many winged nightmares. Flying over the melee, they swooped down into the fray on the ground from time to time.

Terror gripped Dalton, knowing that the cliff loomed up behind him and he was hemmed in by a horde of the battle-maddened entities. His gaze met those of the other hardened souls, their eyes filled with a frenzied madness.

A particularly tall entity shoved its way through the crowd. Brimming with muscularity, its appearance was as bestial as it was human. To Dalton's eyes, it looked as if human elements were fading into something primal.

The entity gazed upon him with blood-red eyes. It pointed a talon-ended finger towards him with an accusing air.

"You sent a great many upon the path to war. The spirits you darkened, the seeds that were sown, the blood that was spilled ... you have earned a great reward. Here on this great battle plain you may revel in the essence of war, in all of its glory," the huge figure sneered at him, with an edge of triumph. Reaching down, and clutching Dalton, it jerked him up from the ground with little effort.

"Rejoice with us and celebrate, oh lord of war! Your domain has been waiting for you! Welcome home!"

Thrust high into the air, Dalton could see into the far distance, in every direction. The barren plains and its fighting occupants seemed limitless, as a terrible despair took hold of him.

There was no way out, and nowhere to try and run. He could not hide anywhere on the heavily congested plain. For the first time in his existence, Dalton felt the icy absence of hope.

He gazed skyward, and everything within him cried out. On a scale reflecting a being of immense size, a face, beautiful and cold in expression, could be seen within the churning black and gray cloud-mass.

Unquestionably majestic, and entirely inhuman, the being's luminous eyes reflected great pleasure in Dalton's severe plight. He knew he beheld the master of the realm he was within, and also realized that no manner of pleading or appeal would sway the regal figure. Quite simply, mercy had no place in a realm harmonized fully with the truth of war.

The beast-thing holding him aloft boomed with laughter, unceremoniously flinging him through the air. Dalton's body arced towards the waiting hands and claws of combatants filled with bloodlust.

The horrors that he endured rivaled those he had witnessed and been threatened with. He was torn limb from limb in the most literal sense, only to find himself somehow reconstituted, to experience something similar again.

Other times he was battered and pulverized, his flesh and bones pulped by the pounding fists of irresistible assailants. The fury of war was visited upon him over and over, and only maniacal laughter met his screams.

Each single instance seemed to last forever, and deep down he knew that the suffering would never end. The scale of his life's own debt was staggering to comprehend, and there would be no rest in a place where time had no dominion.

He had been a lord of war, and now he would experience its essence in the purest, clearest way forever. No elaborate ceremony, well-pressed uniforms, shiny implements of technology, or cheering crowds were there to obscure the true face of war. Seeing the visage of war in all of its raw, unrestrained fury, Dalton could only shriek and scream as he was lacerated and shredded apart yet again.

***

"Dalton? Helen? What in the world are you two doing here? And where the hell am I?"

The haughty, caustic figure that had been his Secretary of Defense through two terms was no more. In his place was a man with a hollow, lifeless stare; the kind of faraway gaze that has beheld indescribable horror.

The president's brow furrowed, immediately sensing the sharp difference in Dalton Rockefeller. A sense of unease draped over the president, as he knew something was terribly amiss.

"So good to see you, Mr. President. We have been waiting for you to arrive," Dalton greeted his former boss, in a voice that held no trace of enthusiasm.

The president's eyes shifted towards Helen Carville, who gave off the same leaden air as Dalton. In a word, she looked empty.

"We have been waiting for you, most of all," Helen said, in an even, emotionless tone. This time there was a smile on her face, though it was frigid and lacked any trace of goodwill.

A well-built, young-looking man then stepped forward, his sudden presence causing the President to flinch in surprise. He could see immediately that both Helen and Dalton were deferential towards the martial-looking figure, who could have been any one of the men in his personal security.

With an iron-hard look in his eyes, he addressed the president, "You will understand all of this very soon, Mr. President. You have cultivated on a great scale for many years."

A seed of dread sprouted and began to grow within the president's spirit. There was something very unsettling about the tone of the other man, almost as if he were passing a sentence upon the president himself.

"Cultivated? What are you talking about?" the president replied, trying to keep his voice confident.

"Why yes, quite a cultivation it has been too, Mr. President," the figure replied. "You have quite a harvest awaiting you in this place, sir ... and abundant harvest ... as do all lords of war."

ABOUT THE AUTHOR

Stephen Zimmer is an award-winning author of speculative fiction, whose works include the Fires in Eden Series (Epic Fantasy), the Rising Dawn Saga (epic-scale Urban Fantasy), the Harvey and Solomon tales (Steampunk), the Hellscapes tales (Horror), and the Rayden Valkyrie tales (Sword and Sorcery).

He is also a writer-director in moviemaking, with feature and short film credits such as Shadows Light, The Sirens, and Swordbearer.

Further information on Stephen can be found at www.stephenzimmer.com

Transcend reality with Seventh Star Press!

On the following pages we would like to introduce you to some of our titles featuring Sword and Sorcery, Post-Apocalyptic Fantasy, Epic Fantasy, YA Fantasy, and more!

To get more information on Seventh Star Press and our titles, please visit:

www.seventhstarpress.com

or connect with us at:
www.twitter.com/7thstarpress
www.facebook.com/seventhstarpress

Grand Epic Fantasy from Stephen Zimmer!
Explore the world of Ave in the Fires in Eden Series from
Stephen Zimmer! Epic Fantasy for those who enjoy authors
like George R.R. Martin and Steven Erikson!

Softcover ISBN: 9780982565612

eBook ISBN: 9780982565698

Softcover ISBN: 9780983108627   Softcover ISBN 9781937929855

eBook ISBN: 9780983108610   eBook ISBN 9781937929862

More from Stephen Zimmer!
The Rising Dawn Saga, a series that explores the
dystopian and the apocalyptic!

Book One: The Exodus Gate
Softcover ISBN: 9780615267470
eBook ISBN: 9780982565674

Book Two: The Storm Guardians
Softcover ISBN: 9780982565636
eBook ISBN: 9780982565681

Book Three: The Seventh Throne
Softcover ISBN: 9780983740247
eBook ISBN: 9780983740223

The Rising Dawn Saga titles feature
cover art and illustrations from the
award-winning Matthew Perry

Also available from Stephen Zimmer!

Enjoy action-driven fantasy adventures in the world of Ave in Stephen Zimmer's *Chronicles of Ave, Volume 1*.

Softcover: 978-1-937929-30-5
eBook: 978-1-937929-31-2

Explore the horror stylings of Michael West!

Featuring illustrations and cover art by the award-winning

Matthew Perry!

Trade Paperback ISBN: 9780983740209
eBook ISBN: 9780983740216

Trade Paperback ISBN: 9781937929718
eBook ISBN: 9781937929725

Trade Paperback ISBN: 9781937929954
eBook ISBN:9781937929831

Trade Paperback ISBN: 978-1-937929-18-3
eBook ISBN: 978-1-937929-19-0

16 Tales of the Paranormal and Ghostly
from editors Alexander S. Brown and J.L. Mulvihill!

Softcover ISBN: 978-1-937929-12-1

eBook ISBN: 978-1-937929-14-5

From the shadowed realms of the paranormal comes 16 chilling tales that dwell in the South and South West. From 16 authors, learn of haunted homes, buildings, landmarks and roads where restless entities from beyond the grave desire acknowledgement amongst the living. Become acquainted with the aftermath of an eclipse that awakens the dead in a Memphis cemetery, see what horrors dwell in the woods at Hell's Gate, learn the dark secrets of Sidney's Cotton, and dare to travel down Ghost Road. These and many other tales are sure to keep you awake as you are introduced to what makes the South and South West so unique.... History and GHOSTS!!!!! So, sit back, dim the lights and prepare yourself to face the spirits that walk among us.

The Angelkiller Triad from H. David Blalock!
A series that fuses the digital realms with those of the
supernatural, in a world where in the beginning... evil
gained the upper hand.

H. David Blalock

The Angelkiller Triad
Featuring cover art and interior illustrations by
the award-winning Matthew Perry

Softcover ISBN: 9781937929732

eBook ISBN: 9781937929749

Softcover ISBN: 9780983740230

eBook ISBN: 9780983740285

Vampires Don't Sparkle!

A Seventh Star Press Anthology from editor Michael West!

eBook ISBN: 978-1-937929-69-5

Softcover ISBN: 978-1-937929-60-2

Vampires Don't Sparkle! poses the question: What would you do if you had unlimited power and eternal life?

Would you...go back to high school? Attend the same classes year after year, going through the pomp and circumstance of one graduation after another, until you found the perfect date to take to prom? Would you...spend your days moping and brooding, finding your only joy in a game of baseball on a stormy day? Or would you...do something else?

The authors of this collection have a few ideas; some fanciful, some humorous, and some as dark as an endless night.

Join us, and discover what it truly means to be "vampyre."

www.ingramcontent.com/pod-product-compliance
Lightning Source LLC
Chambersburg PA
CBHW070017260626
47159CB00005B/1848